ABOUT THE TRANSLATORS

KATHRYN PHILLIPS-MILES and SIMON DEEFHOLTS studied Romance Languages and Literature at University College of Wales, Aberystwyth, and later at Birkbeck College, University of London. They have enjoyed varied careers including teaching, translation, lexicography and finance and have spent several years living and working in Spain. They have jointly translated a number of plays for the Spanish Theatre Festival of London as well as the three works comprising the Spanish Season (2017) in the Peter Owen World Series of literature in translation: *Nona's Room* by Cristina Fernández Cubas, *Wolf Moon* by Julio Llamazares and *Inventing Love* by José Ovejero.

OTHER TITLES IN
THE WORLD SERIES
SPANISH SEASON

Julio Llamazares, *Wolf Moon* (translated by Simon Deefholts and
   Kathryn Phillips-Miles)
José Ovejero, *Inventing Love* (translated by Simon Deefholts and
   Kathryn Phillips-Miles)

PETER OWEN WORLD SERIES

'*The world is a book, and those who do not travel read only one page,*'
wrote St Augustine. Journey with us to explore outstanding contemporary
literature translated into English for the first time. Read a single book
in each season – which will focus on a different country or region
every time – or try all three and experience the range and diversity to
be found in contemporary literature from across the globe.

Read the world – three books at a time

3 works of literature in
2 seasons each year from
1 country each season

For information on forthcoming seasons go to www.peterowen.com

NONA'S
ROOM

Cristina Fernández Cubas

NONA'S ROOM

Translated from the Spanish by
Kathryn Phillips-Miles and Simon Deefholts

PETER OWEN
WORLD SERIES

WORLD SERIES SEASON 2 : SPAIN (CASTILIAN)
THE WORLD SERIES IS A JOINT INITIATIVE BETWEEN
PETER OWEN PUBLISHERS AND ISTROS BOOKS

Peter Owen Publishers
81 Ridge Road, London N8 9NP, UK

Peter Owen and Istros Books are distributed in the USA and Canada by
Independent Publishers Group/Trafalgar Square
814 North Franklin Street, Chicago, IL 60610, USA

Translated from the Spanish *La habitación de Nona*

Paperback ISBN   978-0-7206-1953-9
Epub ISBN   978-0-7206-1954-6
Mobipocket ISBN   978-0-7206-1955-3
PDF ISBN   978-0-7206-1956-0

A catalogue record for this book is available from the British Library.

Cover design: Davor Pukljak, frontispis.hr
Typeset by Octavo Smith Publishing Services

Printed by Printfinder, Riga, Latvia

GOBIERNO   MINISTERIO   SECRETARÍA
DE ESPAÑA   DE EDUCACIÓN, CULTURA   DE ESTADO
                Y DEPORTE   DE CULTURA

This work has been published
with a subsidy from the
Ministry of Education, Culture
and Sport of Spain

'Reality is merely an illusion, albeit a very persistent one.'

– Albert Einstein

CONTENTS

Nona's Room

My sister is special. That's what my mother told me at the time she was born in that bright and sunny room in the hospital. She also said, 'Special is a lovely word. Never forget that.' I've never forgotten, of course, but it's more than likely that the scene I've described didn't happen in the hospital but much later in some other room and that Nona wasn't a newborn or even a baby but rather a little girl of three or four years of age. Who knows? I've been told that it could be a false memory and that our unreliable minds are full of false memories. I've also been told that you don't usually notice certain singularities (that's what they call them, singularities) to begin with. All that and the fact that when she was born I was too young to remember anything makes me think that it must be an invented memory or something even more subtle, manufactured, as You-Know-Who would say. Because my life was very different before Nona came into the world. I don't remember it very well, but I do know it was different. I've got loads of reasons to think that it was better, too. Much better. But once Nona was born things changed for ever, and that must be why I got used to thinking that my mother said those words the day she came into the world. That's the day when I started a new life as well. My life with Nona.

To tell you the truth, I would have preferred a brother, but it didn't take me long to settle for Nona. She looked like a doll when she was little. She had very smooth skin, slanted eyes and full lips. When she was asleep her eyes disappeared into a single straight line, and she used to open her mouth and keep it open for ages, as if she couldn't close it or she was about to tell us something, even though she couldn't yet talk and it would take her much longer than most babies before she spoke her first words. I loved her mouth. It was so big and fleshy. Granny loved it, too. 'She's got Brigitte Bardot lips,' she said one day as she sat beside the cot. 'Brigitte is a film star from when I was younger. She's a French actress.' Granny was really happy, and she liked to look on the bright side. So, some time later when Nona finally began talking and we realized that she couldn't roll her Rs properly in her snuffly voice, Granny smiled and shook her head. 'Just like Brigitte,' she said. It's probably because she was so sure and because the smile never left her face that I fell for it hook, line and sinker and did the stupidest thing in my life. At school, that afternoon, I proudly told everyone that my sister was French and she was special. I mentioned it quite a few times – in class, at playtime and on the school bus. I must have bragged about it a bit too much because a few days later some friends came around to my house to play and asked about her. I called her over and straight away, just by looking at their faces, I understood several things all at once. First, Nona wasn't French and, more to the point, the word 'special' didn't necessarily mean something good.

There are only about three years between me and Nona, and until she was four years old we used to play together and sleep in the same room. Then something happened that changed everything, and I turned into the little sister. Nona started snoring.

She ate a lot. She ate voraciously. They put her on a diet, so she raided the fridge at night. She also kept food in her new room in a kind of secret pantry, and even though we searched and searched her room for it we never found it. She was constantly chewing and cramming food down her throat, and she didn't just get fatter (as my parents had feared), she also got taller than me. I didn't like that. No one in my position would have liked that, particularly as it had the immediate effect of turning *me* into the little sister, the hand-me-down girl. From then on any clothes that were too small or short for her were passed on to me. How embarrassing.

You-Know-Who says my parents really messed up with that. (Perhaps I'll tell you about You-Know-Who later.) Although people didn't waste their money on luxuries back then and passing things down in families was quite normal, they should have thought about my age. Once again, he's quite right. After all I was still a little girl, too. Just a child who protected her sister until everything changed. It wasn't simply that we were now sleeping separately in our own rooms or the extra weight that Nona had put on or her sheer size. I sometimes think (and then quickly wipe the thought from my mind) that Nona got fat on purpose in order to distance herself from me, to get ahead of me or to make fun of me because all the changes coincide: the new room, the constant eating, snoring at night and withdrawing into her shell. Everything happened at once, and I had no time to take it all in. The worst thing of all was that she gradually turned her room into a separate world and I didn't mean anything at all to her any more. She turned me into a stranger, a nuisance. 'No entering my room without knocking,' she said once. 'Don't even think about it.' She said it in that odd accent of hers without rolling her Rs. 'No entewwing my woom'. She must have had such a burn-ing desire to make herself understood that this time she didn't even bother to hide her impediment. Nona never used the word 'dress', for example, but rather 'outfit'; she never said 'bedspread' but 'quilt'. The words 'grass' or 'grassland' weren't part of her vocab-ulary; she used 'meadow', 'field' and 'lawn' instead. Her arsenal of alternative words was amazing and proved once again, just in case it wasn't abundantly clear, that my sister had always been very clever – 'special', as my mother used to say.

Mum always took Nona's side; even she knocked on her door before going in. She did persuade her not to lock herself in and, whether she was at home or not, to let Crispi the cleaning lady into her room once a day to clean and make the bed. Nona had no choice but to agree, but once she could do all that by herself Crispi was only allowed in once a week for general cleaning. When she was at home Nona would sit down patiently waiting on a bench outside her room. If it was a school day the first thing she would do when she got home was to shut herself away in there. I imagine she would then carry out an inspection and check that all her things were in the same places she had left them. I imagine, because you can only imagine what went on inside her room. I often used to rap on her door and push it open, sometimes all at the same time, catching her by surprise, but all I managed to glimpse was Nona's face, trance-like, dreamy and lost, as if she wasn't really in her room but far, far away on another planet. Although she reacted straight away and blinked her slanted eyes, for just a few seconds I had caught her in that faraway secret world of hers she didn't want to share with anyone. Then she came down to earth. She was good at coming down to earth, at breaking off from her train of thought, accepting that an intruder had desecrated her sanctuary and acting as if nothing had happened. Pretending.

'Leave her alone,' my father told me one day. 'She's happy in her room with all her things. Don't bother her.'

I had to keep quiet because I knew what would come next: the whole litany of all Nona's qualities and how I had to behave like a model older sister by being patient, considerate and caring. Then the same old sign-off. That frightening afterword, the reminder that Mum always managed to slip in with a smile. 'After all, you're the reason she was born.'

Now I know it wasn't down to me. It was pure coincidence, but they tried to make me believe it, and for a while I did. I was proud of it. I told all my friends what they'd told me I'd done (and that I'd almost forgotten). I told absolutely everyone. One day they took me to church. I saw a statue of the Virgin there, a very beautiful Virgin with a baby in her arms, and I suddenly put my hands together and started praying. I copied the grown-ups: hands together and speaking softly. Later, when they asked me what I'd asked the Virgin for, I resolutely replied, 'A little brother.' I do remember that, or, rather, I remember Mum going all gooey-eyed, the big hug she gave me and what she said. 'Well, I wouldn't be surprised if the Virgin granted you your wish.' And she did, but I didn't get a little brother, I got Nona. Then, time after time, Mum would remind me that Nona was born because I'd asked for her. 'She did the right thing so that you wouldn't be jealous,' You-Know-Who told me one day. 'So that you'd be involved in teaching her.' Rubbish! I was never jealous of my sister. It was the other way around. When she was little and looked like a doll, I used to spend hours and hours with Granny beside her cot watching her sleeping. On the other hand, he could be right about the other thing because I do try to teach her things even though she doesn't let me. She hasn't let me since she suddenly got taller and fatter and I turned into her little sister. I sometimes think that I've got a bit of a grudge against her because of everything that happened, because my friends made fun of me when they saw me wearing Nona's cast-offs and Nona wearing brand-new clothes. But only sometimes, because I scrub those thoughts from my head straight away, and if they don't go completely I talk to him, to You-Know-Who, and he listens to me with a smile on his face.

You-Know-Who has got a name just like everyone else, but I prefer to call him You-Know-Who. All I'm doing is following the family tradition. In our house we give our own names to different things. I don't know who started it, but there are lots of words we simply don't use and some other worse words that are completely forbidden. Once, a lady, a friend of the family, stroked Nona's hair then waited until she left the sitting-room and blurted out one of those words. She's never been back. Mum gave her a dirty look and asked Crispi to see her to the door. We don't want to hear anything about foreign surnames or diseases or calamities and even less about things said in whispers or to see pained expressions. Here, everything is special. Whether you like it or not. Just like Nona herself. That's why, because she's a special girl, we take her to a special school as well. Special people have their own singularities. I said so before. Singularities. It's a word I've known since I was small, and once I could use a dictionary I understood it even better. Because singularities (which means more or less the same as 'characteristics', 'peculiarities' or 'oddities') go very well together with special people. It is only to be expected. You're special because you have singularities. Or you have singularities because you're special. It's all a bit circular. Like the way whiting is sometimes served, curled around so the fish bite their own tails. The other day Crispi made them for lunch, and I stayed in the kitchen for a while to watch. I thought it was a good way to explain the world. At least in a way. Nona was the whiting and the circle made by putting the end of the tail in its mouth was her room. You can't understand one without the other and vice versa. I watched as Crispi carefully put the tails between the fishes' teeth and how she skilfully squeezed the heads to make sure the tails would stay there. Then she dusted them with flour and fried them two at a time so that they wouldn't stick together. Then she put them on some kitchen paper to soak up the oil and finally placed them in a china dish garnished with slices of lemon and a few sprigs of parsley. I would have stayed in the kitchen much longer thinking about all this, but you have to eat fried whiting straight away, whether they're biting their tails or not. You have to eat them before they get cold. And that's what we did. I sat down at the dining-room table and carried on thinking about Nona. I thought that my sister was like a dragon protecting its treasure, circling every part of its lair and not letting anyone see inside. I also thought that if I could release the pressure of the teeth on the tails an opening would be created, a door or a crack through which you could enter the forbidden room and discover all its mysteries. My parents were eating heartily, and soon there was nothing left in the china dish but the garnish of slices of lemon and sprigs of parsley. I didn't tell them what I'd been thinking about. Just in case. They might have thought it was funny, or perhaps not, which would have been worse. But I would tell You-Know-Who. I would tell him that my parents had swallowed up their own daughter (just a joke) and how I thought the whiting and my sister Nona looked like each other – that was the important bit. You can tell You-Know-Who almost anything. I like that. But that's also why I have to protect him and protect myself. I don't want anyone to go searching around in my things, discover his real name and start putting two and two together and bothering us. So I keep him secret. Just like his photograph. In school the other day while we were talking in the small classroom that is sometimes used as an office, I thought of taking his photograph. I asked permission, of course, but I didn't tell him the truth. I was embarrassed. I didn't tell him he looked really handsome in his light-blue polo shirt and that I was desperate to have his picture on my mobile for ever. Instead I told him that I was doing an end-of-year project and needed silhouettes and backlight. He smiled and stood up and went and leaned against the window, and I clicked the shutter. It wasn't a silhouette that came out, of course. He came out, which is exactly what I wanted. Nona's got her big secrets; well, so have I!

We know very little about the special school. At least, I don't. Nona doesn't really let on anything about what she does there, but I don't think she likes it very much. When she comes home each day her face lights up when she gets to her bedroom door. In she goes and doesn't come out again until dinner time. What on earth could be in that room to make her so happy? When I'm in bed I sometimes put one ear to the wall and wait for a while. Apart from snoring Nona sometimes talks in her sleep. She talks to herself, and recently we've heard her laughing a lot, as if something very funny was happening and she was having a great old time. I've known she's had a boyfriend for a while now, or perhaps it's a girlfriend. I'm not sure. Mum told me one day when we heard her talking to herself. It's an invisible friend or the imaginary friend that children who feel lonely sometimes make up; an only child, for example, or children whose brothers and sisters are much older and don't want to play with them. According to Mum it's not a bad thing, in fact, the opposite, as it encourages creativity. There are even some famous artists who had imaginary friends when they were small.

'It really isn't a bad thing,' Mum says again to convince herself.

Sometimes I think that Mum isn't very convinced either and like me wonders why on earth Nona needs an imaginary friend. She's not an only child. She's got me, and if she doesn't play with me it's because she doesn't want to. What is more, she's growing up really quickly. I don't get her cast-offs any more. Mum realized her mistake years ago, and although Nona's more developed than I am and is still taller than me we each dress in our own individual style. We don't even look like sisters. A school friend told me just the other day, 'You and Nona don't look like each other at all.' I don't know why, but I liked that. Then I felt bad about it. She's my sister after all. But the truth is that Nona is special, very special. She behaves as if she's angry with me, as if she wants nothing to do with me, as if I'm a drag. Sometimes when I'm listening to her laughing on the other side of the bedroom wall I think that when it comes down to it she's got a great life. I don't laugh as much as she does or have such a good time in my bedroom. There's more. When I had my ear to the wall for a little longer than usual the other night I discovered something. Nona was talking, but she wasn't alone. I listened more carefully than ever, and although I couldn't understand everything they were saying I could make out several voices and different types of laughter. There was a lot of laughter. For a while I thought Nona was a fantastic actress and could imitate different voices. Then I didn't think about it any more as I fell asleep. The next day, as soon as I woke up, I remembered what I had discovered and thought up a good explanation. Nona didn't have an imaginary friend. She had a whole group of imaginary friends! That was it. Nona had a whole gang who had a brilliant time together and that was why she didn't need me. She didn't need me or anyone else either. That was a Sunday, and as we usually did on Sundays we went to see an uncle and aunt who live out in the countryside. We sunbathed and swam in the swimming-pool, and what happened there in the pool really frightened me. We were all drying ourselves off with the towels, and only Nona was left in the water. She was laughing and splashing her imaginary friends. She went down under the water, shouted at them to leave her alone, and she was laughing, laughing, laughing. But that Sunday I noticed something odd. It was more than odd; it was impossible. The water was splashing and making waves all over the swimming-pool as if it really were full of people. And if that wasn't enough (and this is what really scared me) Nona was still laughing and shouting when suddenly her entire body emerged out of the water. 'Bwutes,' she shouted, still laughing. 'You bwutes!' She only appeared for a few seconds and then lost her balance and fell back heavily into the water. But I immediately knew she couldn't have managed that feat on her own. It was as if I saw a whole host of hands and arms lifting my sister up by her feet. Once the joke was over those hands, arms and feet splashed about in the water again all over the place. They do exist, I said to myself, worried.

Her friends really do exist. I was about to call out, but I stopped dead. My eyes met Nona's slanted eyes, and I immediately saw her mechanically waving a hand and looking very serious. It was just how she looked when I caught her in her room when she was far away and she'd had no choice but to come back down to earth and pretend that she hadn't been found out. I'm not entirely sure what she meant by that mechanical wave, but I can guess who it was meant for. The water gradually became still until there were just some ripples lapping around Nona as if nothing had happened.

When we got home in the evening I waited for the best time to talk to my parents. Dad folded up the newspaper he'd begun reading and went out of the sitting-room. At first Mum listened to me attentively.

'A gang? Well, that's not such a bad thing.'

That spurred me on. It was difficult to explain what I'd found out. I couldn't find the right words, and when I thought I had found them they didn't ring true to me. But I plucked up courage. It was too serious to keep quiet about it.

'Yes, a real gang. There are loads of them. We can't see them, but they *do* exist.'

'Of course they do,' she said smiling. 'That's what imaginary friends are for, and when children grow up real friends take over from their imaginary friends. It's always like that.'

I realized that it was all going to be quite a lot more complicated than I had thought. So I started at the beginning: the voices coming from Nona's room the night before and the riot she and her friends were creating in the swimming-pool that morning.

When I got to the bit when Nona was hoisted up out of the water the same thing happened as before. My words didn't ring true, and I didn't know what to say and kept quiet.

'And?' she simply said. But I had the feeling she was getting impatient.

'They lifted her up,' I suddenly said, and even I was surprised by my decisiveness. 'I couldn't see their hands because they're invisible, but I could see Nona's ankles. On the surface of the water. Like an apparition, a virgin or a saint, although she's neither of those things. It was them. Her friends. Do you understand me now?'

My mother shook her head and shrugged her shoulders at the same time. She was saying yes and no at the same time. I just had to carry on to the end and tell her what I had realized when I was wrapped up in a towel beside my aunt's and uncle's pool. To lots of people my explanation would seem crazy, but not to me. There was a reason I'd started shivering that morning, and it wasn't because I was cold.

'They could be aliens from another planet. Beings that we can't see but Nona, or children who are as special as Nona, can. Or perhaps they're ghosts. Children who died ages ago and who have come back into the world to play with Nona.'

I stopped there. I couldn't do anything else because Mum was looking at me furiously. I'd never seen her like that.

'That's enough!' she said, and now she was extremely cross. 'Enough of that! I've had just about enough of your imagination!'

Then she left me on my own in the sitting-room in exactly the same place where I'd gone to ask for help, to tell her what I'd found out. A little later I could hear her arguing with Dad in another room. They'd argue sometimes but not very often. Mum spent her time reading. Books and more books, essays, especially papers on psychology. Dad was interested only in the newspaper and sport. But they got on well together, really well. That was the first thing You-Know-Who asked me at the beginning of the school year. Do your parents get on well? Yes, very well. I think I added, although they don't always agree. This was one of those times. They didn't agree. They were arguing, but I didn't even try to listen to what they were saying. I felt hurt and upset. There's nothing worse than telling the truth and no one believes you. Or they think you're joking. Or they refuse to listen to you, which is what had just happened to me. So I ran to Granny's room. Granny, whom I love so much. She looked as happy as ever and so understanding, sitting in her rocking-chair with her lovely smile.

'Granny!' I shouted.

And I threw myself into her arms. I told her about the voices I'd heard on the other side of the wall, about all the splashing in the swimming-pool, about my eyes meeting Nona's, that more than anything else. Our eyes meeting. My eyes wide with fear meeting Nona's slanted eyes and her suddenly understanding what I had just realized, what I had found out. And that when she waved it was just a reflex reaction. As if she were batting away flies or flicking away something nasty or as if she were saying 'That's enough! Enough! Stop it!' The gesture was a lot like an order, a strict warning from a person used to giving orders and being obeyed. And she did it. She made those beings – aliens from another planet or dead children – stop playing and splashing about in the swimming-pool, and all of a sudden the water became still and the only ripples left were the ones lapping around Nona.

'She's the queen of a kingdom we can't see,' I shouted.

Granny was still smiling, and she stroked my hair. I buried

my head in her lap, and we both rocked in silence. Granny can't talk. She hasn't been able to talk for a long time. She can't move either, but she's never lost her smile. I love her more than anyone else, and I feel safe in her lap. Perhaps that's why that day I clutched her so tightly that the rocking-chair started creaking. Or groaning. Or grumbling. It was as if all of a sudden Granny, the rocking-chair and I had fused into a single being and into a single grumble. Because the see-sawing of the rocking-chair on the wooden floor made a noise that repeated a name.

Nooonaaa, Nooonaaa, Nooonaaa. It never changed. Nona.

The next morning I thought about the whiting. The whiting that Crispi had so expertly made a few days ago for lunch, biting their own tails. I thought about everything they had called to mind then and especially about the idea of finding a crack or a door that would let me into the forbidden room. But now I realized that I didn't need to release the pressure of the teeth on the tails to create an opening and break the circle. There was no need at all. If the whiting was Nona and Nona was the dragon protecting its treasure, all I had to do was to evade her watchful eye and slip into her lair as calm as you like. I also realized that the reason I hadn't thought about this before was because it wasn't easy to imagine her room without its permanent occupant. For me, it was as if Nona spent her whole life there. She was at school when I was; we left home and came back at pretty much the same time. So whenever I was at home Nona was already *living* in her room. It was the same thing every day. Even though we might have met at the front door or come in together hand in hand in the hallway, a few seconds later Nona would shut herself away in her kingdom. But the time had come for things to change. That very day. All I had to do was to wait until the time, just like every day, the dragon went to school, Dad went to the office, Mum went to the library and Crispi took Granny out for a walk. Then on the way to school I would turn around and go back home.

Going into her room without knocking was strange at first. We had all got used to knocking on the door, although we would open it straight away without waiting for a reply. That's why we always surprised Nona, distant, withdrawn, lost in her secret world. But it was different today. There was no one guarding her lair. So I went in without knocking, and although Nona wasn't there I could smell her: that strange mixture of medicine and eau-de-Cologne. Nona's smell. I opened the cupboard and searched the drawers. I wasn't surprised that everything was clean and tidy, as that was the strict condition for Crispi not going into her bedroom any more than was agreed. Then I sat down on the bed. Nona was doing an excellent job all on her own. The sheets were beautifully smooth, the pillows plumped up and the quilt didn't droop over any corner more than it should. I went over to the window and opened it wide. Her bedroom looked even more clean and tidy in the morning sunlight but more impersonal, too, more unremarkable. Then I wondered what exactly I had been expecting to find and couldn't find. But I didn't know the answer.

If it weren't for Nona's unmistakable smell – which impregnated the sheets, the furniture and the curtains – that room could have belonged to anyone. There were no clothes out of place and not one single personal object. There was nothing to explain why she enjoyed being shut away within these four walls. But I wasn't fooled for long. I gradually started to understand. I reminded myself that in her own way my sister was clever, very clever indeed.

I realized that I was simply seeing what she wanted me to see: a room just like so many others; a bedroom with no personality; a room that only came to life when the owner came back from school and took up her rightful place again. Because Nona brought her room with her wherever she went – along with her friends, the gang of friends who had been splashing around in the swimming-pool the day before and would no doubt now be waiting silently for her outside the classroom, sitting on the benches in the corridor, invisible to everyone else and desperate to get back home so there would be no more obligations and no need to pretend. Yes, Nona, the queen of the gang, was very clever, and her room simply told me what she wanted it to tell me: nothing.

I closed the window so that everything would be as it should be and was about to leave when I noticed a light flashing on her computer. I went over to the desk, hardly able to believe my luck. It was a miracle. Nona had stopped halfway through a session on the computer, and, even better, had forgotten to shut it down. I pressed any old key and the screen lit up. Then I did get nervous. But I can't remember if that was right at the beginning, because I felt that what I was about to do wasn't right at all, or if it was later when I realized that I'd just gone into the Pictures folder and a whole mosaic of photographs and drawings became available to me at a click of the mouse. And that's what I did. I clicked on Slideshow and, half nervous, half amused, watched a procession of film stars, models and athletes on the screen. There were only boys, many of them bare-chested, in swimming-trunks or leotards. They were all handsome and some of them were muscular and robust as well, proudly showing off their healthy bodies or bulging biceps. They were blond, dark-haired, black, white and mixed-race boys. There were all kinds in Nona's album.

'My little sister. Who would have thought it . . .' I said out loud. Then almost immediately I went red, out of annoyance, surprise, embarrassment. I went red and froze the last picture in astonishment because in that endless procession the one person I would never have expected to see had just appeared. It was someone posing, smiling, beside a window in exactly the same position as the photograph I had taken at school. But now he wasn't wearing the light-blue polo shirt that matched his eyes. He wasn't wearing a shirt or a bathrobe or a tracksuit either. It was You-Know-Who on Nona's computer screen. Completely naked. Smiling.

After the shock I understood immediately that as well as being clever Nona was evil. Really evil.

He has a real name, as I said earlier, and it's not a secret any more. Nona has written his name in red below his photograph. She's also included his job: psychologist. You-Know-Who is the school psychologist. He's a young man who has just left university and has new ideas about treating patients. Some children at school agreed to be volunteers so that he could work on these ideas and put them into practice. Then we can all learn. He can learn from us and we can learn from him. I love telling him things and listening to him. He likes listening to me and talking about my life. I sometimes exaggerate a bit, as you have to tell him everything. I exaggerate about how annoying Nona is and how difficult I sometimes find it to be a special child's big sister. But if I do exaggerate it's only to please him. We see each other once a week in the small classroom that's sometimes used as an office. As soon as I open the door, there he is with a big smile. 'How are things

going with your sister?' he asks me straight away. I'm almost
certain he's writing a book. It's a book all about me or perhaps
about the relatives of children or teenagers like Nona. He knows
how much we have to put up with and how much we have to
sacrifice, but I don't think there's any way he could possibly
imagine Nona's latest dirty trick.

Because that's what it is, a dirty trick. I don't know when she
got hold of the picture, which I've always kept safe with me on
my mobile. She clearly stole it when I wasn't looking, put it in
her album and, with the worst intentions in the world, started
touching it up. If I looked carefully and enlarged it I would be
able to see what she had done. You-Know-Who's face, the
classroom/office window and the naked, muscular body that
didn't belong to him and which had been layered on top. There
was a definite change of colour on his neck, and it was precisely
there where she had deleted the blue polo shirt and replaced it
with someone else's body. But there was something that was worse
and completely inexplicable. How did she find out his real name
and his job? Once again you can see how clever she is (finding
it out) and how evil she is (writing it in under his photograph).
It was as if she were saying to me, 'You can't have any secrets from
me. I'm the only one allowed to have any secrets in this house.'
And for once she wouldn't have mispronounced her Rs and so
wouldn't have needed to find alternative words. She was just
perfect. Increasingly so. Just like the idea of leaving the Pictures
folder on her computer open knowing that one day I wouldn't
be able to resist having a look through her things and spying on
her. One day, or even that very morning. How could Nona know
everything? Sitting in front of the screen, breathing in the smell
of medicine and eau-de-Cologne, I suddenly lost it completely

and I hated her. I hated my sister. I realized that I'd always hated her, and that while I was ashamed of her I was jealous of her, too. I realized that I would have liked to have met her gang and share their secrets. I realized that I couldn't stand the fact that my parents believed her and doubted everything I told them. That's why I stood up and bashed in the computer with the chair legs and smashed the screen. I turned the drawers upside down, threw her clothes all over the floor, messed up the bed and stamped on the sheets. I opened the window again and broke the glass. I was in such a fury that I didn't notice the sound of the door or the creaking of Granny's wheelchair.

'What's been going on, darling?' I heard all of a sudden.

I turned around with a start and saw Crispi looking scared, not daring to come into the room. It was too late to make up excuses and blame aliens from another planet or dead children.

'Nothing,' I replied in tears. 'She deserved it.'

All of this happened just a short while ago, but it seems like ages. Crispi phoned my parents, and they came home quickly. They arrived together and were arguing. Dad was in a bad mood. He said, 'I knew something like this would happen', and added that if it had been sorted out when it first started, 'I wouldn't have to leave the office halfway through the morning.' Mum told him over and over to be patient. But when they came into the room and saw me sitting on the floor in among the broken glass she was the one who lost control. She pulled me up by my arm and forced me to my feet. 'We're going to have a serious talk,' she shouted. Her voice was strange. She sounded furious and as if she were about to burst into tears, all at the same time. She dragged me into the sitting-room. All three of us sat down. Mum and Dad were on the sofa, and I sat down opposite them in a wing-backed chair. Dad was still in a bad mood, and Mum was taking deep breaths as if she was building up her strength to speak.

'Why did you do that?' she said eventually.

I shrugged my shoulders. I couldn't tell them the truth this time. I couldn't tell them that Nona wasn't quite as angelic as they thought and about her collection of photographs of boys. I particularly couldn't tell them how she'd made fun of my only secret, how she'd humiliated me and humiliated him. There are some things you can't tell your parents. It's just too embarrassing. Besides, I wasn't sure if they'd believe me. Just like the last time; like always. So I kept quiet and shrugged again.

'If you've got something to say, then out with it,' said my mother. 'If not . . .'

She didn't finish her sentence. An unspoken threat was left hanging in the air. I didn't know what she meant and started trembling, and they soon started arguing again, more than ever, as if I wasn't there. They never argued like that when I was there. The only choice I had was to step in.

'Apart from being clever, Nona is evil,' I said, 'really evil'.

And although I was horribly embarrassed I didn't give them time to react and told them what she'd done to You-Know-Who's lovely picture. She'd stolen it, touched it up and included it in her collection of photographs of boys. There's more. I didn't call him You-Know-Who but used his real name so there could be no doubt. So that they'd know I was telling the truth. I also promised them that the next time I saw him I wouldn't tell him anything about what had happened, but my parents had to know.

'Do you mean —?' My father mentioned You-Know-Who's

name, and I nodded with my eyes glued to the floor. Then he turned to my mother. 'Isn't he her psychologist?'

Mum stood up and took my head between her hands. 'That doesn't make any sense, sweetie,' she said in her softest voice. 'The doctor is a respectable elderly gentleman, a prominent figure.'

I shook my head, but she held me tighter.

'He's an imaginary friend.'

'Another one,' my father groaned.

'A handsome, young imaginary friend, and you've given him the real doctor's name and job.'

I wasn't going to argue any more. What did they mean? Did I have imaginary friends just like Nona? It was all a big mess. I took my mobile out of my pocket and tried to find the photograph. Not only had Nona stolen it she'd deleted it as well.

'This has gone too far,' said my father – but he wasn't talking to me; he was talking to Mum. 'And as for you, on top of everything else, it was you who said imaginary friends aren't a problem, that they help some children discover themselves, you said, creative, sensitive spirits . . . Don't you see what you've done?'

I don't know if she saw anything because she was looking at me with her eyes glazed over, as if she were blind or lost in her thoughts. But at that very moment I did start to see, to go back in my mind and join together sentences and recall certain moments. I began going over the constant bickering with my sister and listening to Mum repeating over and over again, 'After all, you're the reason she was born.' Always the same old words. And me telling my friends a story I only half remembered. The story of a girl in church one Sunday morning praying like the grown-ups and asking the Virgin for a little brother. Someone to play with, someone to take away the loneliness of being an only child. But was that really true? Had it really happened like that? And why do I remember Mum looking at me a bit sarcastically as if she didn't believe it all, as if it were a personal joke between the two of us, a bit of mischief? For the first time I wondered what she really meant. And what she had really meant just the day before. An accusation. A complaint. 'I've had just about enough of your imagination!' I felt shivers down my spine. An electric current that shook me from my head to my toes. Once, twice, three times . . . I don't know how many times. Until, waking up from a dream-like state I thought I understood. I squeezed Mum's hands, and she was still looking at me, glassy-eyed.

'Now I understand everything,' I said. 'What you said, why I'm scared. I understand that perhaps you're right and You-Know-Who is nothing more than an imaginary friend. But he's not the only one.'

I noticed her hands were cold, and I squeezed them even tighter between mine. The heart-stopping moment had arrived. I was scared, but I had to tell her.

'Nona doesn't exist,' I finally said. 'That's right, isn't it, Mum. Nona doesn't exist?'

The light came back into her eyes. They really lit up, accusing me. They were burning into me.

'Stop turning things around to your own way of thinking,' she said in a tired voice. 'Of course she exists!'

My father walked out of the sitting-room looking dejected. All of a sudden I was frightened. Really frightened. I felt as if I were in the middle of a terrible nightmare, as if I had already experienced that situation before that morning, but I couldn't remember the ending. Perhaps there wasn't an ending. Then Mum squeezed my hands until they hurt, so that I couldn't leave, so that I would listen to her with undivided attention.

'Accept it for once and for all,' she said very seriously. Then, without releasing the pressure on my hands, making sure I couldn't escape, she added slowly, very slowly, 'She is the *only one* who exists.'

That was the ending, the ending I couldn't remember, the ending that pursued me when I was asleep. The eternal nightmare. But then, when I woke up, everything was back in its proper place and things went back to how they were before. This is what I told myself, 'Be patient. When you least expect it, it will all be over.' I said that to myself a short while ago, just a few moments ago, but now it seems like an age. I tell myself the same thing again without really believing it because I know today is different and it's not a dream. Mum is still clenching my hands and has just dug a nail in. I don't know if she's done it on purpose or didn't mean to do it. But I don't wake up. I can't wake up. Today isn't a dream. So I shake her off with kicks and slaps and rush down the corridor. Granny's there in her wheelchair with the permanent smile on her lips. I guess that she's been listening to everything we've been saying, immobile in her wheelchair. For that reason and because she always sees the good in things, I crouch down beside her and plead with her, 'Granny! You tell me. If she's the only one who exists then who am I? What's my name?'

Granny moves her lips. She wants to speak but can't. She gestures to me to follow her, and her bony hands turn the wheels on the wheelchair. She stops suddenly and points to a door. As I don't move, she turns around and looks at me. It's the first time in my entire life that I've seen her looking serious and not smiling. And, something I would never have expected, two tears are silently rolling down her cheeks. I notice that a solitary tear, on the right-hand side, is rolling down much faster than the other. But then it stops and the tear on the left-hand side overtakes it. It looks like a competition. A race. I don't know which one to bet on. The right-hand tear spreads over her skin and disappears, but then unexpectedly a reinforcement rushes down from above. The left-hand tear, on its own, is just about to reach the finishing line, Granny's chin, when the end of the race speeds up. Granny has dried her eyes with a handkerchief and has just wiped her face with it. I end up not knowing which tear won. She points to the door again. I open it and smell medicine and eau-de-Cologne. I notice that the floor is clean, the drawers closed, and if it weren't for a breeze coming through the broken window panes no one would believe anything had happened there. I close the door and turn towards her. Was that what she wanted to show me?

I don't like the expression on Granny's face. She's looking serious and is still pointing at the door with a trembling finger. And I'm afraid once again. I'm afraid of what her glaring eyes are silently telling me. I'm afraid of what's always there at the bottom of everything I do and I no longer know whether that's when I'm asleep or awake; I'm afraid of the images that have always pursued me since I was a child and that I do my utmost to escape. This morning Granny doesn't seem to want to protect me. Neither does Mum seem to want to repeat, as she always does, 'Well, it's only a game. That's how you learn.' Perhaps one of these days things will get back to normal and how they used to be. But not today. Today, I have no choice but to *accept* it. I have no choice but to answer the question 'Who am I?' as Granny would have done a moment ago if only she could speak. Just like Mum has already come up with an answer in her own way and Dad, too, leaving the sitting-room, dejected, leaving us on our own. '*You* are no one. You're just Nona's projection. An invention. Her imaginary sister.' These words pierce my very being like daggers, and I can't defend myself. But I control myself. I take a deep breath, push the door open and go resolutely into the sanctuary. It's one way of acquiescing. 'I know that I'm Nona!' It's also a way of stopping everyone interrupting me for a while so that I can get my thoughts together. I don't feel afraid or upset any more. All of a sudden, just after coming in, I feel certain that this situation isn't new either. I've experienced it before. Not once but several times. I just need to wait it out and to remember that after the storm comes the calm. I just need to concentrate, and there's no better place for that than in this room, my room. Everyone knocks before coming in and there are no mirrors. There is no surface that would dare to reflect back fleshy lips or slanted eyes. I am the person I want to be. So I close my eyes, take a deep breath and I wait to escape from a body I don't recognize. I wait to see things from the outside. I'm waiting for my family to calm down and for the waters to recede gradually.

Then, as always, I'll have so many things to tell You-Know-Who.

Chatting to Old Ladies

She had arranged to meet her friend at the Bar Paris at seven, but she got there half an hour early. The marble table by the window was free. That was a good sign. She ordered an espresso with a shot of milk then immediately changed her mind – a whisky would be better. Andrés was her only hope. Her last and final hope! She took a large gulp to bolster her spirits. There was no going back now and no beating about the bush when he arrived. She would get straight to the point. A peck on each cheek, then in for the kill. 'I need some money.' Before he could say a word she would explain the situation coolly and calmly. 'I'm in a bit of a fix. I'm being evicted tomorrow. You've got to help me.' She would show him the eviction notice and wait, not for long, just long enough for him to realize that it was serious. As soon as he said, half taken aback and half annoyed, 'Oh dear' or 'That really is a problem' or, more likely, 'We haven't seen each other for two years and you drop this bombshell on me', she would hand him pen and paper. 'It's just a loan. I'll sign a contract. You decide on the terms and conditions and tell me how you want me to repay you.' Andrés had always been kind. And at one time, as far as she remembered, he'd had a bit of a thing for her. She shrugged. It felt cheap. It was cheap of her to phone Andrés, put on her tightest jeans and her silk blouse carefully unbuttoned to reveal her cleavage. But there was no other option. He'd seemed friendly enough on the phone. 'What a surprise, Alicia! How's it going?' She hadn't told him how it was going but simply said, 'That's what I want to talk to you about. Why don't we meet up?' She'd tried to speak as calmly as possible, without being overdramatic and not letting on that she was desperate. She'd managed to pull it off. After hesitating for a moment Andrés had suggested meeting at the Bar Paris. 'At seven. I won't have much time. You've caught me on the hop.'

At half past seven she was still sitting all alone at the marble table by the window. At a quarter to eight the waitress came over carrying an empty tray. 'Are you Alicia? Somebody phoned and left a message for you. The person you're supposed to be meeting can't come. He said to give him a ring next week.' Alicia paid for the whisky. Four euros fifty. She left a tip of ten cents and counted the rest of the change. Five euros forty. It was all she had left in the world. She left the bar and took a deep breath. Bastard, she thought. That's Andrés for you. A cowardly bastard. She buttoned up her blouse. And as for me, I'm just a slut.

She crossed the road and stopped in front of the window of an espadrille shop. She hated the sight of her own reflection. She deserved it. Getting all dressed up for Andrés, having such faith in her charms, taking it for granted he would sort things out for her. She felt humiliated, not only by Andrés but also by the agent and the two-faced landlady. 'Don't worry, Alicia. Pay me when you can. We were all young once.' Just thinking about the landlady made her blood boil. What a cow. A con artist. A bitch. Stringing her along like that – 'Don't worry . . .' – then letting that Rottweiler of an agent loose on her. Threatening to repossess the flat. Imminent eviction. A masterpiece of deception. Get rid of the tenant and stick the rent up. Bad luck had something to do with it, too. Just a few weeks before she had been certain her television series would be accepted. She'd been working on the script for over a year. It was almost a done deal. Then a new manager came along and her whole world collapsed. It had served her right for trusting to luck and being so naïve.

'Can you give me a hand?' said a voice behind her.

She turned around, irritated, and saw an old lady wearing a flowery dress smiling at her. She looked like she wasn't short of cash.

'I'm diabetic and sometimes can't make out different colours. Are the lights on green or red?'

'Green,' said Alicia.

She needed a hand, she thought. A hand . . . that poor woman needed a hand as well. 'I'll walk you across,' she said and took her arm.

The old lady smiled again.

'That's so kind of you, dear. I live close by.'

She was right outside the Bar Paris again, and the old lady still had hold of her arm. They walked on a little further.

'Thank you, thank you very much. I live just here.'

Alicia felt a little better. A good deed is its own reward. Just for a second she had managed to forget all about her own problems. She looked at the building. The entrance had seen better days, but at least the old lady had somewhere to live.

'Would you like to come in and have something to drink?'

Poor woman, thought Alicia. She's all alone and needs someone to talk to. She's even more trusting than I am, inviting a complete stranger into her home.

'I'm sorry,' she said and looked at her watch, 'I'm meeting some friends for dinner.'

She'd been fantasizing all morning about what was going to happen that evening. After getting over his initial shock Andrés would give her a cheque or they'd arrange to meet the next day, first thing. In any case, he would cancel his engagements and invite her out to dinner. A friend in a fix deserved all his attention. But nothing had come out as she'd planned. Five euros forty cents . . . that was all she had left in the world. Her last chance had been and gone, and all she had left was five euros forty cents.

'Another time then,' said the old lady as she took a bunch of keys out of her pocket. 'I'm Ro, Rosa María, but everyone has always called me Ro.'

Alicia thought Ro was charming, a charming old lady.

'I'm on the fifth floor.'

Alicia imagined what the fifth floor was like. There would be an enormous flat full of keepsakes. It would be a flat typical of the Ensanche district. There would be the dining-room and a glazed veranda at one end and the master bedroom at the other. There would be a long corridor, which Ro would struggle up and down a thousand times a day. Ro, she said to herself. Now she thought about it, her last chance was actually Ro.

'OK, I'll come in for a bit. Just for a bit.'

Ro's face lit up. She opened the door and pressed the button to call the lift.

'The fifth floor,' she repeated.

All was not lost. Ro seemed so happy that, who could say, if she told her all about her problems . . . She wouldn't give her money, no. Old ladies don't like letting go of money, but they do like having company. She would be sure to offer her a room and insist that she come to live with her, for a few weeks at least. She had no one else to go to. She would be out on the street the next day. Unless, perhaps . . . She thought of something awful. So awful and shameful that she hated herself for all she was worth. But it wasn't a real thought. It was more of a vision. A subliminal image. Money. Banknotes hidden away in strange places, in the kitchen next to the rubbish bags, in the bathroom in among the rolls of toilet paper. Old ladies were like that. They hid away anything of value and then forgot all about it. They usually had jewellery, too. Alicia briefly remembered her grandmother. 'Come here, dear. I'll show you my jewellery.' A few days after she died long-forgotten banknotes started popping up in the most unlikely places.

'Well,' said Ro. 'Make yourself at home.'

It was a large flat, crammed full of things and a little untidy. Alicia followed the old lady down the corridor to the dining-room. It was dark, and the curtains were drawn. The old lady turned on the light and asked her to sit down.

'What's your name, dear?'

'Alicia'

'That's a lovely name!'

Ro really was charming. She opened the door to a 1950s sideboard and took out two small glasses and a bottle of sherry. Alicia felt awful again. Robbing old ladies – it was even worse than trying to seduce Andrés. She would have a glass of sherry and leave.

'I like to have a chat with you young girls sometimes. Would you like a biscuit?'

She opened a tin and carefully arranged half a dozen biscuits on a china plate. Alicia took one. She hadn't eaten anything since that morning.

'Come and see me whenever you want. I don't go out much, and you'll always be welcome.'

She really was a kind and pleasant old lady. Perhaps she would pay her another visit sooner than she expected. The next day, with all her luggage and anything she was allowed to take out of the flat.

'What about you, Ro,' she said, rushing her sherry. 'Don't you feel like you're rattling around in such a big flat?'

'Oh, no!' The old lady burst out laughing. 'I'm used to it . . . although you're right, it is big and I do lose things sometimes . . .' Then she looked around, searching for something.

'Can you do me a favour, dear, and help me find my glasses. I put them down somewhere just a moment ago – on the sideboard perhaps.'

Alicia got up. As soon as she found the glasses she would ask her. A mutual favour. The old lady treated her as if she had known her all her life, and the flat was huge. One room. All she needed was one room. Just for a while.

'Here they are,' she said.

Suddenly, with the glasses still in her hand, she stopped dead in her tracks. She had just seen a wooden bowl on the sideboard in between the yellowing photographs, the little silver boxes and the porcelain flowers. It was a salad bowl with the words 'A souvenir from Mallorca' written on its side, and it was crammed with rosaries, wrist-watches, buttons, a pile of old copper coins and – was she dreaming? – several five-hundred-euro notes.

'Thanks again. Would you like another biscuit?'

Five hundred euros! There weren't many five-hundred-euro notes in circulation. Perhaps the old lady didn't know how much they were worth or she'd forgotten. But, there they were, in the wooden bowl, jumbled up together with all the trinkets, rosaries and useless coins . . . There were at least five or six of them. Perhaps more. Six times five hundred . . . It was almost what she owed. This really was her last and final hope. Tomorrow, before they threw her out of the flat, she would pay it all off. She wouldn't be stealing; it would just be a loan. She would pay it all back as soon as she could, down to the last penny. She would pay it back in instalments, leaving the money in the old lady's letter box, in an envelope, with no return address or signature as she would never see her again. Although . . .

'Alicia,' said Ro, 'are you all right?'

Alicia. She had made the mistake of mentioning her name. That proved she had no intention of stealing from her, but it was a clue. She remembered the waitress in the Bar Paris asking her, 'Are you Alicia?' An old lady accusing someone called Alicia and a waitress who remembered passing on a message to a woman called Alicia. That idiot Andrés! Not only had he stood her up he had also told everyone in the neighbourhood who she was.

'Yes, Ro. I'm all right. I smoke too much and sometimes . . .'

'I'll go and get some liquorice sweets for you. They're good for sore throats.'

The old lady disappeared down the corridor, and Alicia took a deep breath. It wouldn't be stealing, she repeated to herself; it would just be a loan. No one had seen her going into the flat. The building didn't have a concierge, and they hadn't seen any of the other residents. Besides, who would believe the old lady? Five-hundred-euro notes on display in the dining-room for all to see? Quite likely she didn't even remember they were there. Didn't she say she was constantly losing things? Ro would forget her name just as she had forgotten all about the small fortune in the bowl. She had to be decisive. Now! She got up and took the banknotes. Seven of them – salvation! She put them in her pocket.

She didn't have time to go back to her chair. She thought she heard the old lady's footsteps and bent down, pretending she had a problem with the heel of her shoe. She saw a broken doll and a teddy bear without any eyes on the floor.

'I can't find them,' said the old lady. 'I'm sure I bought a bag at the chemist's yesterday.'

Alicia showed her the teddy bear.

'Have you got any grandchildren?' she asked.

She spoke clearly, naturally, as if she had nothing to hide.

'No,' said the old lady. 'My son hasn't got any children.'

A son. Would her son know that his mother had a small forgotten fortune in a bowl? That she offered sherry and biscuits to any old stranger?

'Does your son come and see you often?'

It was a polite farewell. Alicia was picking up her handbag and getting ready to leave the flat. The last thing that mattered to her at that point was whether the old lady's son did his filial duty.

'No,' said Ro, 'he doesn't come and see me. Why would he have to come and see me?'

She didn't see her expression. The old lady had turned around and was holding the edge of the curtain that separated the dining-room from the veranda.

'My son lives here. With me.'

Everything happened in the blink of an eye. She whipped the curtains back and the clinking of the curtain rings merged into her last words. 'Here. With me.' Alicia's eyes clouded over. What was that? She had to lean against the back of a chair so as not to fall over.

'This is Alicia,' she heard.

A large, deformed man was staring at her from behind iron bars, slavering at the mouth. He was a monster. A beast. A giant. He had a bulging head, expressionless eyes, and his face was covered in pustules. Alicia's handbag was the first thing to crash to the floor, quickly followed by Alicia herself. The next day when she woke up she remembered that the last thing she'd heard was Ro's voice saying, 'Be gentle with her, son. Real-life dolls are very delicate.'

But it couldn't be real. It wasn't real. It was just a horrible nightmare. The worst dream imaginable. Alicia was in bed, and her eyes were still closed. She heard a key in the lock. 'They didn't even bother to ring the doorbell,' she murmured. 'OK then, throw me out. Evict me! Anything is better than . . .' She suddenly felt a rough hairy hand and woke up with a start. It was daytime, but she wasn't in her room between the sheets of her bed. Instead, she was sprawled on a straw mattress inside a huge cage. Ro had just opened the door and put down a tray on the floor. She didn't even look at her.

'I'm off to church, son.'

Ro left the barred veranda and turned the key in the padlock.

'Let's see how long this one lasts you. It's getting more and more difficult to find someone. Young girls nowadays, they're all sharp as a button and they don't like chatting to old ladies.'

Before the curtains were drawn Alicia spotted the wooden bowl on the sideboard. The five-hundred-euro notes were there along with the rosaries, the buttons, the pile of copper coins, her wrist-watch . . . She didn't want to see any more. She closed her eyes and could smell his stinking breath close to her mouth. She wanted to die. But the giant man had already lifted her up in his arms and was rocking her from side to side. Just like a baby. Just like a much-loved doll.

Interior with Figure

It's not a large painting, barely twenty-eight by thirty-five centi-metres. What is more, the frame they've used makes it seem even smaller. The first time I came to see the exhibition I almost walked straight past and missed it. There was a tall, burly man completely blocking my view. He had a neck like a bull and a curious way of stretching it like an adjustable reading lamp. He also had a massive head, and he leaned forward very slowly as if he were waiting for the moment to lunge at the painting. So I carried on with the guide in my hand: *Macchiaioli: Impressionist Realism in Italy*. I stopped in front of a Signorini, discovered artists such as Fattori and Abbati and was filled with admiration once again for the perfect lighting at the Fundación Mapfre. But then, instead of leaving, I went back on myself. I often do this. When I go to an exhibition I usually follow a route, go back on myself and then take up the same route again with all the information I've managed to gather on the way. It's a little like a compressed letter N. And that's how I got lucky. When I came back the burly man with the bad eyesight had gone and I could now look at the painting *Interior with Figure*.

I will try to describe it. There is a room containing only essentials: a bed, a bedside table, two chairs, wallpapered walls. Through the half-open door we can see another door. And there is a girl beside the bed kneeling or crouching down. She's a strange girl.

She's wearing a severe black smock with a little white collar. Her head is leaning against the bed and her hands are holding a bundle or sack that she's probably made herself out of a sheet. We know she's got something inside it because it's bulky. Or docs it just contain dirty laundry? There's a stool beside the girl, or perhaps it's a side-table, and there's an open box on it that looks like a sewing-box. So perhaps the girl has put some sewing she was working on inside the bundle? Table linen or curtains that she's embroidered herself? It's possible. There's a story concealed in the painting, and we'll probably never uncover it. But if we take a closer look it seems as if the girl isn't really kneeling or crouching down. She's huddled up. Or maybe she's hiding from something or someone who could come in through the door at any time. What is more, she's probably so frightened, and still clutching the bundle tightly, that she's closed her eyes. If she can't see, no one can see her. Poor thing! I said earlier that she's a strange girl, and she is. She's more than strange, she's special. She reminds me of a character in a short story I wrote recently whom I called Nona. I walk up to the painting slowly, much like the bull-necked man earlier. This girl, just like my character, has slanted eyes. Or perhaps they're not really slanted. It's simply because she's so bound up in trying to hide that she's got them as tightly closed as she can. Her hairstyle looks wrong for the period, too. She's got short hair with a hint of a Mohican over her forehead. And her ears. I noticed her ears the first day. They're enormous, far too big for a girl. They bring to mind gnomes, elves or imps. Although it's not clear whether that was the painter's intention. Her face doesn't have any clearly defined features. The wallpaper pattern and the brass-and-iron bedstead are both more clearly defined. It suddenly occurs to me that she might not be a girl but, rather, a young woman, and it's only the vast size of the bed that makes her seem like a child. And also the severe dress makes me think of a governess. But, no, I don't think so. She has a child's body, and were it not for the white collar I would say she's a girl in deep mourning. Or perhaps it's some kind of awful uniform and she's in an orphanage? I have the same doubts as the first time around, and I'm more and more intrigued.

Because here I am again in Madrid one week later. I've been invited to take part in a literary workshop, and I'm staying an extra night so I can go and see the Macchiaioli exhibition again. I'll go back to Barcelona later today by train, which is how I like to travel. But for now I've got the whole morning free. Perhaps I'll be lucky and there'll be someone standing in front of *Interior with Figure* giving a commentary on the painting and revealing the secrets of a story that I haven't been able to discover in any book and not on the internet either, nor by naïvely asking an employee who replied by shrugging. So, I don't know any more than I knew a week ago. The artist's name, Cecioni, and the probable date, 1868. Sometimes, like now, I think that Cecioni, who is much more explicit in the titles to some of his other paintings, wanted to preserve the sense of mystery of the room and the girl by being deliberately vague. Perhaps there is no such mystery, or perhaps there is, but the painter, who has been playing around with scale and proportion, would be the first to be surprised at the result. I don't spend any more time thinking about it. I can hear whispering and children's voices behind me. I turn around straight away. A very young guide smiles at me gratefully.

'You can sit down now,' she says to the children.

About a dozen small children sit down on the floor, and I

take a few steps away but don't leave. I like these groups. I like what they do. I like the way the guides skilfully put the period and the costumes in context by pointing out details and figures and how the children, by putting up their hands and asking questions, gradually bring everything to life. It's as if they're colouring in cartoons in a comic. Having fun. Today I'm really curious to find out what the painting means to them. So I wait.

'What a bed!' says one little girl.

All the others are just as surprised. To them, it seems enormous. 'It's old,' says one. 'It's old-fashioned,' the guide corrects him. But no one (neither the guide nor the children) mentions what I thought they would: the story about the princess and the pea and her gigantic bed. Perhaps Hans Christian Andersen doesn't feature in a modern curriculum, or maybe these children pay much more attention to detail than I did at their age. How could you possibly compare a bed with only three mattresses to the sensitive princess's gigantic bed with twenty mattresses! I suddenly feel like a silly grown-up, and for a moment I feel nostalgic for a childhood I never had – these children are able to sit calmly in front of an oil painting and say whatever they wish and not simply what the teachers expect – as in times past. Somehow, without moving or changing my position, I manage to sit down beside them. How old are they? Nine, ten?

'The girl's playing hide-and-seek with some other children who aren't in the painting. She's holding her breath so they can't find her.'

'No, she's not playing. She's a thief. Everything she's stolen is in the sheet. That's why there's hardly anything in the room.'

'And because she's really young and it's the first time she's stolen anything she's a bit scared.'

'She's really scared. She's trembling. But she hasn't been stealing and she hasn't done anything bad. It's because . . .'

This latest comment comes from a redheaded little girl. She's started talking and has then stopped dead in her tracks. She's still staring at the painting, mesmerized, without blinking. It's as if she's not seeing the same thing as everyone else or at least not in the same way.

'And?' asks the guide. 'Carry on, don't be embarrassed.'

I don't think the little girl is the slightest bit embarrassed, but she is upset. I don't know why. She takes a deep breath.

'She knows they want to kill her,' she says finally.

And she's still staring at the painting.

I'm struck by the way she speaks clearly and deliberately and by the way she behaves as well. She's examining the painting as if it were an open book and she's just reading a few sentences. The guide goes back to her work.

'*Who* wants to kill her?

And she's smiling. The guide's smiling, but the children aren't. They're looking wide-eyed at the little girl.

'Her parents,' she says resolutely.

The silence that meets her words will soon turn into a question. And she replies. She doesn't take her eyes off the painting, and giving it her full concentration she speaks clearly and deliberately again and explains what we all want to know. You would think she was talking to herself. The guide isn't smiling any more.

'She's hiding in her room with the door open. She's left it open on purpose so they'll think there's no one in the room and they'll go and look for her somewhere else. The girl's ears look big, but they're not. It's just that she needs to listen carefully in case anyone's coming. Later, when she's sure there's no more danger, she'll leave home and go far, far away. And they won't be able to kill her.'

You could hear a pin drop. I get the feeling that we don't exist. As if we're in a different reality. There's an invisible circle around us, although you can hear the echo of other footsteps and voices. Not only the echo. Now, as if my own ears had got bigger as well, I can clearly hear comments and appreciative murmurs being made in the furthest reaches of the room. But our silence devours them. *Our* silence. I've felt like a member of the group for a while now.

'OK, but why would parents want to kill their own daughter?'

The guide seems slightly anxious. She's losing control and doesn't know how to regain it. Perhaps that's why she starts smiling again, or perhaps she wants the rest of us to think she's smiling. But all she manages is a grimace, a rictus grin, a false parody of a smile.

'Because she knows something. She's seen things she shouldn't have seen.'

'Oh, right.' The grimace looks nothing like a smile now. 'And what has she seen? What things has she seen?'

The guide is young and probably hasn't got much experience. Or perhaps this is the first time she's come face to face with such an interpretation. Her question has slipped out, and now she regrets it. Why on earth has she asked about the *things*? Better not to know.

The redheaded little girl hesitates for the first time. She seems confused, as if she were waking up from a dream. She looks at the floor and answers in a thin voice, 'I can't say.'

And she closes her eyes. Just like in the painting. I'm suddenly aware of a kind of symbiosis between the two girls: the little girl beside me and the disturbing figure dressed in black. They have melded into one another, and there is a similarity that goes beyond the physical. I recall a few moments ago when the little girl was studying the painting without blinking, and it seemed to me that she was *reading* something in it. But now I think of something else. The little girl was looking at the painting and saw herself reflected there as if in a mirror.

'So, she can't say.' The young guide has recovered her composure. 'Let's leave it there. Does anyone else want to say anything? Has anyone got a different interpretation of the scene?'

I don't know if she's misheard her and it's a mistake or if it's the opposite: she's heard her perfectly clearly and she's said it on purpose. What's certain is that in a very loud voice and adamant tone the young guide has just made a significant transference. In a matter of seconds. Because it's no longer the flesh-and-blood little girl who's admitting 'I can't say' but rather Cecioni's figure from her strange position beside the bed who's admitting that she can't say. And if the figure in the painting is refusing to cooperate there's no point going on. Perhaps teaching hasn't changed as much as I thought and anything a bit out of the ordinary is still frightening. That's why the guide is trying to calm the situation down. She points to the children one by one. 'You, perhaps? Or you? Who hasn't spoken up yet?' She's clearly trying to make them speak up and wipe away any trace of the anxiety and bewilderment that was apparent a few moments ago. Finally one of the children puts up his hand.

'He's a boy dressed like a girl.'

There is laughter from the other children. The young guide is laughing, too. They are all roaring with laughter. There's a whole string of guffaws reverberating around the room, which I interpret as relief. I suppose it's contagious. More and more children's heads are shaking with laughter. But I imagine that someone is immune to all this. The redhead maybe? Because her head isn't moving at all. She's not taking part in all the fun, and neither does she pay any attention to the words her fellow pupil comes out with next.

'He's going to a fancy-dress party and has taken his big sister's dress without asking. He's hiding because someone's coming.'

This is the final version, the one that prevails and which the children will all take home with them. The guide seems very satisfied and waves her hand to make the children get up and then sit down again in front of another painting hanging on the opposite wall. I stay behind the group for a short while longer. I listen to interpretations and ideas. But now the little redhead isn't saying a word. I'm not surprised. She's already said everything she had to say at the time in front of *Interior with Figure*. In front of a mirror. Now she's just a little girl keeping a secret.

I decide that my visit is over, and I go into the shop. I buy some prints, postcards, coloured pencils. It's a grey day with a leaden sky, but I want to walk to the Paseo del Prado, collect my case from the hotel and wander down to Atocha Station. I leave the Fundación Mapfre building and walk a few metres. Not far, not even as far as the first corner. Because almost at once I stop dead in my tracks. I've just heard a squealing of brakes followed by screaming. There's a lot of screaming. It is children screaming. And someone urgently shouting – although it's lost among the cars' honking – 'Be careful!'

It's the group again. There are the children standing stock still on the pavement like stone statues. The young guide, kneeling down on the ground, is holding one of them, but I can't make out which one. I go up to them. A woman beside me says it's all right, it was just a scare. A few drivers are still honking their horns. The little boy who had fallen over, still holding on to the guide, now tries to get up with difficulty. He seems to be limping a bit. He's grazed his knees and there's a bit of blood on his leg. 'It's nothing compared with what could have happened,' I hear someone say near by. 'They drive around here like madmen.' 'It's just reckless to take a group of small children out on the street with only one person in charge.' 'The school bus should have been parked at the entrance and not on the other side of the road.' No one knows exactly what has happened. It all took them by surprise. I don't ask anything else. As I understand it, accidents always take you by surprise.

But I don't go just yet. The little boy (I can finally see his face) is blond with freckles and looks scared, then he bursts into tears. The guide gives him another hug. I look towards the other children, who are still standing on the pavement, searching for the little redheaded girl. It takes me a while to find her because she's wearing a red mac with a hood, which she didn't have on when she was sitting down in the exhibition. I can see her trembling. A helpless Little Red Riding Hood who's just heard the wolf's warning. I catch her looking at the little blond boy with freckles with as much concentration as when she was studying Cecioni's painting a while ago. But she doesn't seem mesmerized now. She's just trembling. As if she knows that the accident was meant for her; as if it were just a mistake, a simple matter of time. I remember what she said when she was melding into the girl hiding in her own painting: 'They want to kill her.' Just as the guide did, I change the object of the verb and attribute it to her: 'They want to kill me.' That's what she was telling us earlier, and her eyes, wide with fear, are telling us the same thing again. Or is it astonishment rather than fear? I'd like to be able to read Little Red Riding Hood's mind and find out if she thinks that what just happened was simply a mishap, a failed assassination attempt or a warning of death. Although it actually doesn't matter much. Perhaps the little boy with freckles rushed out into the road without looking and without thinking about the danger. What does matter is the shock. The little girl is trembling at the forewarning of what might happen to her. It's one possible way to get rid of her. An accident.

A police car and an ambulance arrive at the same time. I try to speak to the police officers and paramedics, to tell them that it's not only the little boy who needs some attention. One of the other children is suffering from shock. You can see she's trembling. But I don't get any further than the mandatory 'Excuse me'. They tell me, together with all the other onlookers, to move along, to leave the scene. I can't even get a final sight of the little girl in the mac. A traffic policeman leads the children in a line to the other side of the street to the school bus, which is waiting for them. I have no choice but to go on my way and wonder over and over again what I should I do.

It comes to me as I'm walking along. I noticed when I was out yesterday that there's a police station a few blocks from the hotel. I think it's in calle de las Huertas, or perhaps it's the next one, calle de Moratín. In any case, I've got more than enough time to think about what I ought to tell them. A redheaded little girl, the Macchiaioli, what she said in front of the painting, the sudden squeal of brakes. Ask the paramedics or the police officers. They'll know the name of the school – or schools, if there's more than one, because now I think that perhaps it's an *ad hoc* group on a tour of several art galleries with children from a number of different places. I also wonder whether the young woman is actually a teacher working with some of the children in a particular school or if she's just employed as a guide and doesn't know the children at all. Too many questions. How can I construct a coherent argument with so few facts? I could begin by introducing myself. 'Good morning. I'm a writer. My name is —' But I can't get over how ridiculous that sounds, even in my imagination. A madwoman trying to pass herself off as a writer. Or a mad writer. What difference would it make? To avoid any misunderstandings I could suggest they look me up on the internet. I'm sure they wouldn't do that, at least not while I was there. But even if they did and even if it proved what I'd told them, why would they take any notice? Police stations must be full of visionaries, mediums, obsessive types, the unemployed, housewives with extrasensory perception or people just as imaginative as me. Here's another one playing at being Agatha Christie, that's what they'd think. And, besides, what would the official complaint be? A crime that hasn't yet been committed and a couple I've never met in my life, parents of a little girl with no name. It's not good enough. I could have my excuses ready when I go in. That would be better. 'I know I haven't got enough evidence, but I'd like to tell you about something I've just seen, in case one day . . .' One day what? I don't imagine they have much spare time in police stations or that they would file away simple hypotheses under the heading 'In case one day'. But I carry on, '. . . in case one day there's a suspicious accident, a disappearance, a death, remember what I said and . . .' I'm not convinced by that either. 'Madam, there are suspicious accidents, disappearances and deaths every day.' All I can do is ask them to be patient and to begin at the beginning. The group of children at the exhibition. What the little redheaded girl said, her expression, my feeling that she was talking about herself. The postcards I bought in the shop are in my handbag, and one of them is of *Interior with Figure*. Perhaps it would be a good idea to show it to them and leave it on the desk to explain myself better. But I have to be particularly clear that, in the beginning, at the exhibition, although I was struck by the little girl's words and expression, it was nothing more than that. A little girl with a secret. Nothing more. Until I saw what happened later on outside the building, with the little boy being hugged by the guide and the little girl trembling like a leaf, when I understood that her story wasn't a fantasy. Now the description. Red hair. Between nine and ten years old. Wearing a mac with a hood, also red. 'Now she's telling us the story of Little Red Riding Hood. We'll be on to Snow White next.' No, best not to mention the colour of the mac. Best not to do anything at all, at least as I'm getting closer and closer to the hotel, and to the police station as well as it's on the way, and my imagination starts playing tricks on me. Because the inspector, deputy inspector or whichever cop is dealing with me isn't helping at all. I don't know why I had to imagine him like this: athletic, muscular, disrespectful and wanting to rush back to the gym, which he should never have left. It's probably down to the influence of films or television series, whatever. I feel awkward before speaking, before coming up with some plausible allegation, and I go into the building without being in the least bit convinced and already feeling defeated. Although not all is lost. I want to believe that it isn't. Let's imagine for a moment (one of those coincidences in life) that one of the many police officers in the entrance hall at the time has actually read my books or, at the very least, has heard of me. He may not recognize my face, but he does recognize my name. And once he does he decides to take on my case personally, whatever it is.

So he attends to me. This changes everything. I see myself making excuses again, admitting that I don't have any proof, showing him the postcard of *Interior with Figure*. All very natural and stress-free with the mutual understanding that usually exists between reader and writer. But how would the supposed reader react? He's smiling. The kind and amenable policeman is smiling.

'You're too sensitive. That's why you're a writer.'

No, that won't do me. I would prefer something more professional.

'There's not the slightest bit of evidence. Words spoken in front of a painting and a tremendous scare seeing the little boy's accident. A very emotional little girl.'

Perhaps. But what about what she said about her parents wanting to kill her? Her or the girl in the painting, it makes no difference. And what's the motive? She's seen things she shouldn't have seen. At least that's what she said.

'And haven't you thought about what those *things* could mean?'

Yes, of course I've thought about it, and the teacher or guide did, too. But the thought flashed through my mind so quickly. Now the imaginary cop helps me to recover it.

'It's more than likely that she caught them in bed, at it . . . if you see what I mean.'

Perhaps he's right. The redhead went into her parents' bedroom when she shouldn't have. She's confused the delights of love with force, aggression, a fight to the death. And her father was very annoyed and kicked her out. Or her mother. Or probably both of them because she's accusing them both. *Her parents.* They might have threatened to punish her as well. But death?

'Some little girls are incredibly imaginative. You wouldn't believe it!'

I erase the image of the police officer/reader from my mind. He's not helping me much either. Or maybe he is. Maybe I've been naïvely using him to get used to the idea once and for all. To accept that it's not in the least bit important that on my very first foray I should go through the door of the police station already feeling defeated, indecisive, with no speech prepared, as if everything were lost from the start, because the fact is that everything actually is lost from the start. Not even the kind and well-disposed imaginary police officer has been able to sort it out. 'An imaginative and emotional little girl.' That's all there is to it. Anything else, the possibility that what she might have seen or discovered has nothing to do with intimate bedroom games, is of no interest. Even though (and this is mere supposition) it's so terrifying and embarrassing that it makes her fear for her life.

I walk on. I say to myself that I never really thought seriously about going to the police. And that life is full of illusions and it's so easy to doubt innocent people. Despite the fact that it was only in my own head I'm shocked when I think about what I was planning to do just a few moments before. Believing in a little girl's fantasies and pointing an accusing finger at her own parents. Something completely irresponsible, which hasn't happened and will go no further than my imagination or my thoughts. I'm leaving the Paseo del Prado now and turning into calle de Moratín. That's right, calle de Moratín. I wasn't mistaken. I can see the police station, the door of which I will never darken, a few metres away. There are two police officers chatting in the doorway. It may be an illusion, but from here, from where I am standing, they seem strangely familiar. One of them is tall, arrogant and proud of the muscular body that's taken him hours of work in the gym. In contrast, the other is short and smiley and looks as if he can't wait for the working day to be over so that he can get down to reading like one possessed.

I pick up my luggage from the hotel, a bag I put over my shoulder, and quickly walk towards Atocha Station. When I get there the AVE train is already on the platform. I run like I haven't run for years. When I get to my seat I sit down heavily, exhausted. For a moment there the idea that I might miss the train seemed as if it would have been a complete disaster, the end of the world. How absurd it all is, I think. Now that the train is moving I actually feel liberated. I don't think about the reason why, but it's revealed almost immediately as my hands automatically fold down the table and take the envelope containing the postcards from the exhibition out of my handbag. I quickly go through them one by one until I stop at the one in which I'm interested. It looks really strange now. I spent almost the entire morning in front of the painting, and I'm as struck by the scene as if I were seeing it for the first time. The soulless room, the half-open door, the huddled figure clutching a bundle, the gigantic bed. The bull-necked man who was about to charge at the canvas must have felt something similar. I smile when I remember this and imitate him by placing the postcard close to my eyes for a few seconds before putting it away. But I don't put it back in the envelope. For the last time, and by way of saying goodbye, I recover the image of the flesh-and-blood little girl. I kneel her down beside the bed dressed in her red mac. She's a frightened Little Red Riding Hood once again, and now she's the protagonist in the painting. She's the one who's scared and hiding and planning her escape. And it must be because I'm travelling at the speed of light and Madrid is getting further and further away that I start thinking about the theories

I rejected. And I think about what it was she must have seen that has put her in so much danger. I think about a crime that could only be covered up with another crime. About the way she was trembling. About her panic attack. About how she was certain she was an obstacle or posed a risk. About her parents. A faceless couple in the privacy of their home secretly plotting the best way to get rid of their daughter.

I'm back at the beginning once again. There's no way around it. The little girl is hiding in the soulless room, and now I have no doubt that she really is in danger and she's right to be frightened. I take some paper and a pen out of my handbag. A letter? An anonymous letter? A signed letter in which I will very calmly recount my theories point by point? I know full well that it's useless and ridiculous. But the pen and paper are still on the table beside the postcard as if they were urging me to continue, as if they were waiting for something. Perhaps that's why, taking the top off the pen, I think of a title, 'Interior with Figure', and do the only thing I can do. I start writing a story.

The End of
Barbro

When we were little one of us discovered it was possible to look at something without actually seeing it. It happened one summer's day in a village in the mountains when we were playing with some other children our age and we found a dead cat. None of us three girls had ever seen a dead cat – and definitely not such an enormous one. It was lying in a pool of blood, its eyes open and still like a doll's eyes. But the image lasted only a few seconds because someone yelled almost immediately, and then everyone started running and screaming and out of the large group of children standing beside the blood-red pool only the bravest were left: the oldest boy in the gang and one of us.

Even so, and although it was a long time ago, we're still not really sure which one of us three discovered how to look at something without seeing it. We all think we remember it as if it were yesterday, staring at the cat that had bled to death and our minds lost in the distance, thousands of kilometres away. But one thing for certain is that this modest skill very quickly evolved from being the personal quirk of just one of us to become a skill the whole family shared. We started using it almost immediately in our daily lives. At school, when the classes were particularly boring, we looked as if we were paying attention to maps, explanations, the blackboard or to being told off, and no one ever noticed that we were away with the fairies. We did it so exceedingly well that it was impossible to tell by looking at us. We were there, but we weren't really there. We were proud of it, too, as we are now, as we remember it.

Because we've just remembered it. Suddenly, just like that, a short while ago. And it seems as if we're going to have plenty of time to remember the dead cat, go back in our minds and dwell on any amount of other things from the past, make an inventory of memories or even write a book. The official dealing with us has written down our names and checked them against her list and stared at us (perhaps she was looking without seeing) and asked, 'Are you sisters?' The question is not so idiotic as it might seem. Our first names and surnames are in her papers, but what she really wonders is whether we are triplets. It's strange, as we didn't look much like one another when we were little, but now people aren't sure and get us mixed up, just like the official before she noticed our dates of birth. So we answered, 'Sisters', and she led us into this awful room.

'Take a seat, please,' she said, pointing towards the door at the back of the room with a sign saying 'NO ENTRY'. 'You'll be called in a short while.'

That was already half an hour ago. In that *short while* we've had time to chat, catch up on what we've been doing since we last saw each other, dredge up stories like the dead cat, go all around the houses so that we don't have to face up to the real reason why we're here. And, once again, that reason is Barbro. It is Barbro who's called us to this emergency meeting where, ironically, nothing seems urgent or imminent. But we can't fool ourselves for much longer. That door will open at some point, and we must be prepared for the worst. Although what could the *worst* be?

We don't know.

*

We now think that the worst all started a very long time ago, just like in a fairy-tale. *Once upon a time* . . . it was a fairy-tale that lasted only a single day, but that day was happy, there's no denying it. Barbro, Northern Eyes, came into our father's life when he most needed some love, and that's why we welcomed her with open arms and the best of intentions. Our father was still handsome and had been a widower for too many years. As for his daughters, we were all grown up by then and had careers, friends and our own lives. We weren't at home any more than we absolutely needed to be. We loved him very much, of course we did, but it wasn't the kind of love our father needed. 'I'm a man,' he said to us one day, 'and you can't imagine how much I would love to find the right woman to share my life with.' He wasn't prone to admitting that sort of thing, complaining about being lonely or including us in his plans, but at the time, in spite of that, we didn't attach the slightest importance to what he said. We thought (and later on we would remember this more than once) that he said what he said as an excuse, so that we wouldn't be surprised when, suddenly and unexpectedly, he started going out almost every night, spending a lot of time on the phone or going away most weekends without telling us where. Not only were we not worried, we were genuinely delighted. He'd been a wonderful father, and now it was his turn to have a life. We heard him one evening behind the half-closed door talking on the phone. We thought that he'd joined a club and met up with all his new friends there and that what he'd said about 'a woman to share my life with' was just an excuse, a cover-up. He couldn't find that precious woman anywhere, so he'd decided to have some nights out on the tiles and have a good time.

He lost ten years in a few months. He bought some new clothes and changed hairdresser. One day he announced, 'I want to introduce you to a girlfriend.' A week later he asked us to cook dinner, not a fancy dinner but not too plain either; something between the two that would show off our culinary skills. 'I'm sure you'll like her,' he said with a smile, 'and I'll be proud of my three girls.' That's who we were, his three girls. So the three of us got to work. We made a monkfish-and-lobster *mille-feuille*, pork tenderloin with mustard sauce and homemade chocolate-and-raisin ice-cream. Our father was in charge of choosing the wine, and at nine o'clock in the evening he congratulated us on how beautifully we had set the table. We had understood what he had meant absolutely. Nothing fancy and nothing run-of-the-mill either. The table evoked hearth and home. Yes, that's what he said, 'hearth and home'. Then he looked at his watch. It was the fifth or sixth time he'd looked at his watch. It was as if the minute hand had stopped and time was standing still and only he, with the power of his eyes, would be able to make the watch hands move again. He was nervous and excited, like a small child. We didn't want to ask him what his girlfriend was like, how old she was or where he'd met her. We preferred to wait and see. The doorbell rang at a quarter past nine. Our father opened the door, and there on the doorstep stood Barbro's willowy figure. Back then we didn't refer to Daddy as 'our father'.

We liked Barbro. We thought she was pretty, very pretty. She was casually dressed, and her blonde hair was tied back in a ponytail and she looked at us with her enormous blue, almost transparent, eyes. Her beautiful eyes from the North. Her height proclaimed she was from the North as well. In fact, everything about her screamed the North, with a capital N. Beside her, our father was a fine example of the South, with dark hair, average height, dark eyes and silvery temples; a mature gentleman who still looked good with a young and willowy Scandinavian beauty. Barbro was quite a bit younger than our father, although not young enough for someone to ask if she were his daughter. They made a handsome couple and evoked images of yachts, luxury, endless holidays, international travel and, above all, a second opportunity that had been grabbed with both hands. There wasn't the slightest doubt about that, at least for our father. Wherever she had come from, Barbro was heaven-sent.

'And you are . . .' she said with a smile and trying to put the three names she had only heard of to faces, 'Bel, Luz, Mar.'

She got it right, and we were about to greet her with a kiss but she got there first and held out her hand. She did kiss our father on the cheek, though. We remembered that in many cultures some types of familiarity are limited to family members or very close friends. It looked as if our father already belonged to the latter category.

'It's all really lovely,' she said in a charming accent. 'What a beautiful flat!'

The dinner turned out just as our father had wanted. There was warmth, that feeling of hearth and home that, according to him, began with the table-setting. Barbro praised the wine and tried all the dishes. She loved the monkfish with lobster and asked for the recipe. She said she envied our father because we looked after him so well and congratulated us. We were excellent cooks and adorable girls. He looked happy and was proud twice over: proud of his three daughters and proud of Barbro, too – or, rather, proud of the good impression Barbro was making on his three daughters. Because that's what happened. His Scandinavian girlfriend won us all over from the moment we first saw her, and we understood, without having to ask, that something similar must have happened to him. That was the reason he looked at her entranced. That was the reason his eyes thanked us for the dinner being so successful. We also guessed that barely one week earlier, when he'd spoken dreamily about how much he would love to find a woman to share his life, he'd had to make a big effort to pretend and to hide his happiness. That woman already existed, and her name was Barbro.

We said goodbye, and this time we were the first to hold out our hands, and we said that we should all meet up again soon. Our father called the lift and said he would go down with her. We could hear him laughing behind the closed door and asking her in a louder voice than usual, and sounding slightly tipsy, what she had thought of his three girls.

'My three gorgeous girls,' he said.

'They're lovely,' Barbro swiftly replied, then she added slowly, very slowly and in a half-affectionate, half-teasing voice with an exaggerated accent and tone of admiration, 'Daddy, Daddy, Daddy.'

We didn't want to hear any more. The lift had just stopped on the landing, and, blushing with embarrassment, we left our spying post at the door. We were going to tell him as soon as he got back; he had to conceal his pride and, more than anything, he had to stop calling us his 'girls'. At least in certain circumstances, and the circumstances that night had been particularly special. Did we need to remind him? We cleared away the coffee cups, poured ourselves a drink and waited for him, sitting around that table he'd praised so highly for evoking the feeling of hearth and home. After a while, however, we decided it was best not to mention it and to leave things as they were. After all, he wasn't the first or the last father in the world who adored his daughters, and, joking apart, the best thing was for Barbro to understand that from the off. Then we started laughing. Why were we waiting for him as if he were a small child? And why were we afraid of becoming a hindrance? A hindrance to *what*? The dinner had been a complete success, all the work had been worthwhile, and we felt happy but exhausted. So we called an end to the soirée and went to bed. But that wasn't the end of the story, and none of us could sleep a wink that night.

They got married a week later. It was a very private wedding, held in the utmost secrecy. We were the first to hear about it, not counting the registrar and the witnesses. 'We've just got married,' they said. 'What do you think?' We didn't think it was a good thing or a bad thing either. We weren't happy or sad. They didn't give us time to feel anything either, as after telling us the news the doorbell rang and there was the caretaker. He came in with four suitcases, several bags, an exercise bike and some coats in see-through covers. The poor man made three trips before the lift was empty. And it was then, only then, that we began to understand it all. We understood that we were witnessing a premeditated invasion, that no one had bothered to ask us and that it looked as though our opinion would count for nothing in the future. And we stood there like statues, stunned, speechless. Like statues and lost for words, because statues can't talk and can't feel any emotion. Statues are made of hard and compact mineral substances, just like the three of us that day: three statues standing in the sitting-room. And all the while they were humping suitcases down the corridor, laughing and whispering to each other, cooing like a pair of brooding turtle doves. That was what upset us more than anything and broke the spell and brought us back to life. It was a type of cooing that made us feel embarrassed. It made us cringe. Perhaps it was the first time that we understood what the word 'cringe' really meant. Because of all the cooing and cringing we decided to go down to the bar on the corner. We hardly spoke a word and didn't dare look each other in the eye, but with a few drinks inside us we sorted through our thoughts and memories as if they were scenes from a film fast-forwarding at a frenetic pace and featuring only two protagonists: Barbro and our father. And when we remembered her appearing on the doorstep barely a week earlier it seemed as if years and years had gone by. They weren't the same, and neither were we.

Because on that memorable night barely a week previously everything had turned out just as our father wanted. We liked Barbro. We thought she was pretty, very pretty, with her blonde hair tied back in a ponytail, casually dressed and looking at us with her enormous blue and almost transparent eyes. Her beautiful eyes from the North. But there was something that kept us awake that night and which the following day we put down to being tired, proud of a job well done, all the time we'd spent in the kitchen at the cooker, keeping an eye on the potatoes, or the *mille-feuille*, or in the dining-room selecting the crockery, the tablecloth and the cutlery. That's what we thought at the time, but now we knew it wasn't because of any of that. There had to have been something else that perfect evening, some detail, gesture or word that didn't quite fit. A discordant note, something that grated slightly, something inappropriate perhaps that we refused to recognize because we were so elated. And it appeared in the night disguised as insomnia. Camouflaged. We ordered another drink and carried on picking over the events of the evening. That was what we needed to do. The objective was to determine what it was we'd foolishly brushed to one side when it should have put us on guard. But we also had to cheer up and find enough courage or detachment to go back home and accept that there would be five of us in the apartment, whether we three liked it or not.

It was a lack of respect.

Or perhaps, to put it more accurately, she had trampled all over us. Once we'd got over the initial shock Barbro's presence began to feel unsettling, and in an unexpected way it reduced us to the most degrading anonymity, as if we didn't exist, as if we were non-speaking extras on a stage that belonged to us fairly and squarely. Then our earlier cringing over their behaviour turned into embarrassment over ours, because there are some things you shouldn't think about, and if you do the best thing is to try to forget all about them. But there were three of us, and we couldn't disguise the flash of anger in our eyes. We couldn't resist the urge to complain loudly that our home belonged to us, to the daughters, and that although the law permitted the beneficial owner a lifelong interest it would have been a good idea to discuss it among the four of us. Like always. As we had always done when it came to important matters. But that particular day wasn't *like always*. Infected with so many mad ideas, for the first time in our lives, as daughters, we had pulled out the title deeds to our inheritance and used them as the final argument.

'How embarrassing!' one of us said.

We did feel embarrassed, but our anger and astonishment were even more powerful. We had a last drink and began fantasizing about petty acts of vengeance. What if we asked our boyfriends to move in? What if the flat suddenly turned into a lodging-house, a grotty hostel with four couples crammed into it? What if we decided to practise a dance routine in the sitting-room or set up a percussion orchestra in the kitchen? Not even these infantile fantasies could calm us down. In fact, quite the opposite. As we filled the flat with our friends and imagined the common areas full of kettle drums and maracas, we grew even angrier and more resentful. We ran through the events of the dinner one more time looking for that tiny detail that would explain our father's unexpected behaviour, the hint as to what would happen next. We agreed that they must already have decided on everything before that night. Well, nearly everything. We remembered beautiful Barbro's entrance, with her ponytail, her enormous transparent eyes that grew even bigger as she wandered around the sitting-room and said in her charming accent, 'It's all really lovely. What a beautiful flat.'

Perhaps it was then, at that exact point, when our guest added a detail to what had already been decided. They would get married and live together (all very normal), but they would live together (what a fantastic idea!) in our flat. Nowhere else would do. That's why when we revisited that moment it no longer occurred to us to describe her eyes as enormous and beautiful, blue, from the North (and a whole host of other adjectives) but simply as greedy. We were now convinced that Barbro had been wandering around the sitting-room with greedy eyes.

Was that what we had picked up on without realizing it? We shrugged our shoulders. Perhaps it had been. Perhaps it had not. But if it had been (the alcohol made everything we thought about seem credible) then the rest was easy to imagine. With all her sweet-talking Barbro hadn't taken long to persuade our father. He was an easy catch, much too easy. And the question 'Can a man turn into a fool from one day to the next?' was still floating in the air, although no one took the trouble to answer it because the answer was 'Yes, of course he can'. And he can go off the deep end, too, as we had seen up there in the flat we'd be returning to in just a few minutes. *Our* flat. We didn't feel embarrassed any more, and we weren't cringing either. We were as drunk as lords. We couldn't stop laughing as we left the bar. We went in through the street door, called the lift and went up to the flat. We struggled to put the key in the lock, but when we finally managed it we walked in silently, in slow motion, gesticulating as if we were in a silent film. We stopped at the door to the sitting-room, prudently, selfishly, because we didn't have the slightest intention of having a chat and being polite. We did the right thing. A few seconds later everything fell into place: the reason behind our sense of rejection, the thing that didn't quite fit. A few casual words that should have put us on guard but we'd mistakenly interpreted as having been spoken in jest, a playful joke between lovers, echoing the affection our father had shown towards us. There they were, the two of them. They thought they were alone and hadn't noticed us. He was sitting in his favourite armchair, his eyes were half closed and there was a happy smile on his face. She was standing behind him, massaging his neck, caressing his shoulders and whispering, 'Daddy, Daddy, Daddy.'

She called him 'Daddy' and he called her 'Love'. It was impossible to live with Daddy-Love. At first we avoided the communal areas, the kitchen, the sitting-room and the dining-room, but it was no use. Love and Daddy went through walls. Their laughter filtered through the cracks, and shut away in our bedrooms we gradually saw our dominions shrinking while there were no limits or borders to the rapid advances made by Daddy-Love. The bar on the corner became our new home, and in a way we left the field free for them – but only in a way. We had breakfast there every morning and met there again in the evening. We always sat at the same window table, which looked out on to the street. It was a great lookout point and meant we could keep an eye on the entrance to our apartment block and see who was going in and coming out. That was important. The idea was to avoid bumping into her when she was alone in the flat. This was more than likely as our father worked late in the office during the week. It was even worse than when the two of them were at home. There was no one for Barbro to seduce or dazzle, so she stopped her purring and affectionate caresses and turned into someone else: someone cold, mysterious and distant. On her own, Barbro was frightening.

That was why one afternoon, in an attempt to avoid any unpleasantness, we turned up unannounced at his office. He had to see reason and understand that nothing good could come out of everyone being forced to live together. He had to fix a deadline and start looking for a flat for the two of them. But he completely disarmed us as soon as we saw him. He was happy and smiling and delighted by our visit. For a moment he was Daddy once again. He was a father pleased to see his 'three girls'. 'How lovely,' he said. 'What a surprise.'

He was sincere. And so were we, very sweetly so. We made a superhuman effort so that nothing in our voices would betray the slightest loathing or the least annoyance when we mentioned Barbro. Until we realized it was useless.

'You're not being fair,' he said. 'You're being selfish, too. She's never had a real family until now.' Then, out of the blue, like a medium, like someone reciting something they've learned by heart or passing on someone else's message, he said, 'You three, on the other hand, you've never wanted for anything. I've spoiled you, and I'm ashamed of it.' It had all been an illusion; our senses had deceived us. Daddy had got lost again while that man we called 'our father' had suddenly once more taken on his most recent stage role, that of a possessed and bewitched victim, a puppet operated by his wife: Frozen Eyes.

Thinking about it now, it couldn't all have happened so quickly. There surely must have been some good times when we were all living together. There must have been some moments of mutual understanding and harmony. But however much we delve into our memories we can't find anything to lend any credence to this theory. Once she was married Barbro had cast off the mask of charm she had worn when we first met her. From one day to the next. She didn't even try to hide the fact. She put all her energy into weaving a spider's web around the man we had loved and admired so much. She was his intermediary, his interpreter, his only valid spokesperson. She spoke in his name, gave orders and disagreed with anything we said or did. After all, we were from the South. Even though she had married our father, Barbro sometimes seemed to look down on anything with a mere hint of the South, to such an extent that, apart from being absurd, the situation became grotesque. The North and the South were no longer geographical reference points. They had turned into two opposing teams. The North represented the supreme idea: good; while the South represented ignorance, an absence of the North. Two sides in continuous conflict over any insignificant detail and the inevitable result in favour of the away team. That was the referee's decision, and the referee was our father. It didn't matter whether he was enthusiastic or begrudging. Barbro would look over at us with a flash of victory in her frozen eyes.

We're surprised by it all now. We're astonished and wonder how we could have stood for so much foolishness and why we didn't resort to our old family skill and neutralize her right from the start, to turn her into the dead cat with a frozen stare and, by looking without seeing, transport ourselves thousands of kilometres away. The answer came quickly. It would have been like surrendering, throwing in the towel and leaving the flat to Daddy-Love. It would have been a defeat because, apart from the situation being unacceptable and grotesque, any remaining vestiges of patience and tolerance were being stripped away from us. We didn't procrastinate any longer, and three weeks to the day from when we started living together we went into action, not in the office this time but at home, all five of us together. Our father had to make a choice. It was either her or his daughters. And he did make a choice: his daughters.

All the same, it was nothing like a victory. They had it planned this time, too. They had decided to live in a lovely house in the countryside. It would be ready in a few days. The house also had some land, and they would build a bungalow for visitors. 'You can come whenever you want,' they said later. They showed us loads of photographs. It was the ideal retirement home. And, although the news was encouraging and put an end to the bizarre status quo, something toxic had been floating in the air from the word go: a dark cloud, a portent, proof of carefully premeditated behaviour. A crime scene with her prints all over it. Because we'd had no idea of their plans to buy a house in the country and the wonderful announcement they were going to make, we daughters got ahead of ourselves. This, of course, wouldn't have happened if we'd had any inkling of what was coming, but someone had anticipated how we'd behave. We'd shown our hand too soon, and before we knew it we'd walked into a trap. There was the list of grievances and grumbles that needed an urgent solution. There was also innocent Barbro's feigned bewilderment. She had tears in her eyes, and her face looked like a little girl's. 'I had no idea that us being here was such a problem for you.' Her accent no longer seemed charming. We thought it was false, irritating and artificial. And here she was now, exaggerating her helpless expression and telling us the unexpected news of the move. It was a *surprise*, she said. They only wanted to *surprise* us, she insisted. But she wasn't putting on a little girl's expression any more. Now she was a lamb. A defenceless little lamb being hounded by three bloodthirsty she-wolves. From that day on that's how our father saw us: three she-wolves. It was too late to turn back. We had put our cards on the table, but Barbro had trumped us with a whole deck. The problem was that we weren't able to decipher the codes on her cards. Not yet. Barbro was a box full of surprises, and with her there would always be another 'not yet'.

So, now comes the *coup de grâce*. The joker in the pack. Here we are in this awful room, opposite the door they brought us through a short while ago that led to another door. All we can do now is smile. We're smiling because there was something we didn't understand and couldn't explain, but now we're suddenly beginning to discover a certain mad logic to a mean trick. Because that's what it was, a mean trick. They collected up their things, packed up the best carpets and some of the pictures that had borne witness to our life and left. There was Barbro next to the lift, talking in her innocent and childlike voice. 'I cleared out the office yesterday. It's all clean and tidy. There are just the photos of your mother left.' Did she say 'your mother' or did she dare to say 'your mum'? In any case, it was normal and quite acceptable. What else could she do but leave them where they were? We would go and collect them some time. But not even that, collecting the photographs, was quite so simple. Mum's photographs were waiting for us on the shelves of the old office, that was true. But they were naked, the frames had disappeared, and they were piled up haphazardly, one on top of the other.

It was a fresh tactical gambit from Frozen Eyes. It was vile, contemptible and despicable. We were indignant, but we also started to cringe again. That horrible word: cringe. But now, years later, we're smiling. Barbro, a sometime thief, had stolen the frames. Because they might be valuable? As a souvenir? To run us through with a dagger? 'I hate you. I still don't know why, but I hate you.' She had stolen the frames, and the shadow of the old photographs had gone with them. Because the chain of events that has brought us to where we are now, sitting opposite the closed door that has opened up so many memories, makes us think of something we overlooked at the time: the likelihood that objects have memories. We didn't talk about those things at the time. Now we do, as we have no option. Barbro took the photograph frames to her new house, and Mum's shadow travelled with them. Poetic justice or historical justice. Sometimes it's almost the same thing.

*

We knew a lot about Mum and at the same time not much at all. We knew what our father (when we still called him Daddy) had told us and exactly where and when the photographs had been taken. We also knew, because one of us had reminded the other two, that she liked to read us stories before we went to sleep, how happy and affectionate she was and how much everyone loved her. When she died we were five, four and barely two years old. The eldest boasted about being able to remember the childhood of the other two, the house in which we were born and, in particular, a lot of stories about Mum who, curiously, kept growing in stature with time. Her fantastic memory or our childish desire and imagination did the rest. In our minds 'Mum' was the loveliest thing that had ever happened to us. And there she was, anchored in our heads without any crisis or drama. She was a counterweight who provided us with security, an anchor making sure we didn't lose our balance, particularly at such times as when we discovered the photographs scattered on the shelves. It had shown such a lack of respect, and that was why there would be no reply to Barbro's challenge. There would only be contempt. And to add to that image of the photographs as junk to be discarded there was another one, very similar but at the same time very different. There they were, just for a moment, the offcuts from a film we had not the slightest interest in imagining. It was a television series starring a woman from the frozen North and a man whose free will had been stolen. We weren't bothered about the rest of the plot. We'd had quite enough with the pilot episode. So we collected up the photographs, took them home and gave them back their dignity by putting them in the best frames we could find. As for the rest, we weren't going to lose any sleep over what might happen to the protagonists in future episodes.

The decision was made. It was a defensive strategy, a magical resolution. We shook on it and sealed a pact. We would stick together, just like Porthos, Athos and Aramis, the Three Kings or the Witches of Eastwick. That night the three of us slept like logs.

Without Daddy-Love the flat returned in large part to what it had been before, a mixture of home and headquarters. We stopped resolutely calling ourselves 'we' (as we had begun to do recently) and went back to being Bel, Luz and Mar. We started arguing again, disagreeing about the smallest thing, contradicting one another. It was just as it had been before the Snow Queen came on the scene. It was just as it had been before our father turned into the sad supporting actor in all those fairy-tales that Mum used to tell us and that, thanks to the extraordinary efforts made by the eldest sister, we could still recite by heart: Cinderella, Hansel and Gretel, Snow White. Now, though, they didn't seem like stories but rather astute treatises on human behaviour. We got used to it with time. That's what time can do, turn the absurd into normality. Our father phoned every once in a while and, without fail, spoke about us going to spend a few days with them. But either they never built the bungalow or they didn't really want us to visit. We had only seen the house in the photographs they'd showed us before they bought it and the others they'd sent us after the building works had been completed. We thought it was all normal, reasonable and proper. Although it was a surprise in the beginning, we ended up getting used to having to get past Barbro to be able to speak to our father and also getting used to the people who had once been his closest friends complaining that they had no contact with him at all. Had he been kidnapped or abducted? they asked.

But let's cut to the chase. Time is running out, and the period we're remembering now isn't especially interesting. Nothing much happened during those years. There were the usual arguments among sisters, and distance did away with any other significant problems. We accepted the status quo because it was easier or because we had no choice. The world was riddled with situations like ours. Some were even worse. We couldn't complain. In her own way Barbro loved our father and her own way immediately cut off any other relationship, whether with people who were once his friends or with us, who were still his daughters. Her love was possessive and excluded all others. We didn't know much about her or about her life before she appeared in ours, but there was something that was said a long time ago now, in an office that no longer existed, that gave us an insight. 'She's never had a real family until now.' That was the likely explanation. She had never had a family and hadn't wanted one either. What was more, she hated what she had never had with a passion. And once she had won our father's heart she decided to get rid of us gradually – until our relationship was reduced to sporadic telephone calls, which were increasingly infrequent and increasingly half-hearted. Since they had moved to the countryside we hadn't even spent a single Christmas together. They said they were going to the North. It was the same thing every year. But it was just a half-truth. There was no need to fly or drive thousands and thousands of kilometres along icy roads, as the North had set up home in our enemy a long time ago, and the North lived there within Barbro herself; beside Barbro. We imagined Christmas in a house full of flickering candles, tablecloths with reindeer and sleigh motifs, crowds of guests sampling herring, salmon, mustard-roast ham, mulled wine, saffron rolls. We imagined our father smiling in a corner, full of schnapps and, like a good host, making sure that everything was going well without understanding a word of the babble of languages. We imagined him thinking, even if it were just for a moment, about other far-off Christmases and about his daughters.

No, in spite of everything, we didn't harbour a grudge against him. That would not have been possible. We never stopped loving him, and when one sad day, seven years ago now, he went into hospital at death's door, we hardly ever left his side. He seemed to want to tell us something. He was struggling to trap the words that were trying to escape. He was looking at us with his eyes wide open as if he wanted to warn us, reveal a secret, tell us something of the utmost importance. But we weren't fooled. All dying people do the same. Or perhaps it's us, the loved ones who are desperate to find some significance in their incomprehensible babbling that doesn't actually exist. All that was happening was that he realized he was dying and needed to show us he loved us. He said our names 'Bel, Luz, Mar' over and over again. He smiled and held our hands. In contrast he looked at Barbro with confusion, and once, when she'd just left the room and he could still speak, he asked with his eyes wide open and looking like a little boy, 'Who is she? What does she want? Why does she call me *Daddy* all the time?'

The official has just come in, and she's holding her list.

'I'm sorry. We made a mistake and your appointment was too early, but you can go through soon. My apologies. This time of the year . . .'

And off she goes with the same smile on her face as when she came in.

'It doesn't matter,' one of us murmurs when the woman is halfway down the corridor.

It's true. We don't mind. We're not in a hurry at all now. Quite the opposite. We need to get our memories straight and clarify our ideas. But where were we? It doesn't take too long to pick up the thread again. We were in the hospital, beside the bed, reliving the days when we lost and recovered our father all at the same time. It was a strange time, full of conflicting emotions. It was also when we decided to wipe the slate clean and to support Barbro with anything she needed. He had chosen her; no one had forced him. And she, in her own way, had loved and cared for him. All the same, deep down, we still harboured a grudge. Why had she let us know so late in the day when nothing more could be done? But none of us asked the question. It was too late to do anything about it.

Barbro went back to the countryside with our father's ashes in an urn. She told us she would scatter them in the garden, in the flowerbed where he'd grown his roses with such dedication. She told us about grafting and pruning, fierce battles against blackfly and beetles, about his total commitment, which we would never have believed possible. But she didn't invite us to the ceremony. Perhaps she thought that scattering ashes over the ground wasn't a real ceremony. She did cry, though. She didn't stop crying. In our memories those tears have turned into icicles, although at the time they may have seemed real. We don't know if we were confused back then or if we're mistaken now. And we shrug our shoulders. We're human after all. It's difficult for us to be objective and to recover scenes from the past without being tempted to interpret them in the light of later events. But we're making an effort. We do try. So, let's return to the image of Barbro holding the urn and her eyes full of tears. Let's go back to a serene Barbro a few weeks later with her hair tied back in a severe bun. And back to the day we went to the notary public's office. And back to the various procedures we had to go through that took up most of the following months. We'd never seen each other so often, and, sharing the memory of our father, we managed miraculously to smooth things over. We treated each other with the utmost politeness, almost with affection.

'Give me a few months,' she said as she left. 'I'll let you know as soon as I've sorted your father's papers out.'

We were pleased that this time at least she had stopped calling him Daddy. We were also pleased that she was so willing, without us having to ask her, to go through his documents and give us the ones that belonged to us. And we thought (how ironic) that with his death our father had brought us all the peace he hadn't been able to give us while he was alive. Once again, we were mistaken. Barbro vanished. She vanished into thin air just like in a mystery novel. She disappeared without a trace. She became invisible. She never telephoned once and never bothered to pick up the phone or answer any correspondence. We weren't indignant any more, just fed up. For how much longer would we have to dance to her tune?

We tossed for it; we cheated; we ended up baring our feelings. None of us was willing to go to the village to look for the house we had never been invited to visit, to knock on the door and quarrel with Frozen Eyes. So, once again, we decided that all three of us should go and surprise her. We would be Porthos, Athos and Aramis again, the Three Kings, the Witches of Eastwick. A whole host of trios to which we added a few more along the way: the Three Tenors, the Three Bears, the Three Little Pigs. On the journey we also fantasized about the likely reason for her silence, but we couldn't come up with any that justified such inexplicable behaviour, apart from death. We didn't know how far away the house was from the village, if Barbro got on well with her neighbours or if she was isolated in the middle of the countryside. The address mentioned only the name of a country lane. And that wasn't exactly encouraging. We counted out loud. It had been six months since our first unanswered telephone call, five months since we wrote to her for the first time. It was better not to get ahead of ourselves. Not yet.

We didn't have to search for the house, as it was suddenly there before we reached the village. It looked the same as it did in the photographs. We left the car at the side of the road and started walking along the path without much conviction. Our objective was about fifty metres away, but now, as we were getting closer, something akin to fear was urging us to turn around, to find some excuse, to go back to the car and drive far away. Wouldn't it have been more sensible to go to the police or go to the village and ask around? But we'd almost reached the garden gate. There was no harm in looking, we said to ourselves. Almost immediately after that we heard the soothing sound of a rake followed by the clunk of some stones dropping into something. We ran to the gate and looked through the bars. We rubbed our eyes incredulously. It was impossible. How could the three of us be seeing the same thing?

There he was at the bottom of the garden, raking the ground and piling up stones in a wheelbarrow. He was wearing the old felt hat we had given him years ago and the leather jacket that he had bought himself when he began taking more care with his appearance and started looking younger. There he was, bent over the stony ground, completely absorbed in what he was doing. He had just taken a hanky out of his pocket and wiped his face with it. It was a grim moment in which the hanky wiped away everything we had believed up until then, about our lives and his. Above all, it was as if time had stood still and we might have believed anything. Had we just entered a time warp? Was what we thought we were seeing actually happening or was it just a memory or the ghost of a memory? Unless it was a game, a joke, a trap. In short, a trick. Who had thought up that comedy of appearances? Why? Suddenly, as if he felt he was being watched, he put the hanky back in his pocket, turned towards the gate and looked at us in surprise. It was only then that we realized he was a complete stranger.

He walked purposefully towards us with a hint of suspicion in his eyes. His complexion was similar to our father's and he was wearing his clothes, but there any similarity ended. He was rugged with weatherbeaten skin, and the sun and the wind had left their mark on his face. He carried on looking at us suspiciously, perhaps because of the image we presented at the gate: three young women grasping the bars and studying him in silence. Before he could say a word, we asked him about Barbro.

'The foreigner? She doesn't live here any more.'

We introduced ourselves. He shrugged. He didn't know that our father existed and so knew nothing about his death. He had only seen the foreign lady once. It was the day she left the house, and he'd helped her to load piles of suitcases into the car. We insisted. He shrugged again. He knew even less about the new owners. All he knew was that they were foreigners, too, and they'd asked him to tidy up this terrible garden as much as possible. They'd done it through an estate agent, the same one that the foreign lady had used to sell the house. And that's what he was doing, tidying up all these stones and making it presentable. And if there was nothing else . . .

We didn't even need to look at each other.

'Where did you get the leather jacket from?' one of us said, pointing a finger at him.

It was a decisive event, an accurate shot, a question that reverberated through the air like the aftermath of an explosion. He looked at the three of us, one at a time. There was no longer any suspicion in his eyes, just a mixture of confusion and embarrassment.

'The lady gave it to me,' he said eventually. But he didn't seem really sure about it. 'Well, she asked me to throw away everything in the shed.' There was still silence. 'Papers, boxes, old clothes, useless things.' He opened the gate for us and pointed out a small wooden construction. The famous bungalow? 'I haven't thrown anything away yet.'

An hour later we left the garden. We would never return. It was a garden full of stones and weeds, the earth cracked through lack of water. It was a garden in which lies had been sown, and it was quite implausible that a rosebush had ever grown there.

We're getting caught up in the details again. It would have been better to have started at the end, stopped beating about the bush and talked about the shed straight away. But we haven't seen each other for ages, and perhaps that's why we need to remember, establish the sequence of events and give the circumstances the role they had at the time. Fate, for example. Fate that was beside us from the very beginning, propelling us towards the house at that exact time. The same fate that made the gardener wear our father's jacket and foisted his old hat on him. In short, fate made us turn up on that day when a man dressed as our father was tidying up the garden and the 'useless things' in the shed still hadn't been thrown out.

It's odd that the three of us remember that stranger with something approaching affection. He seems like a borrowed character, someone from a different story, someone sent by destiny to dispel doubts, to save us paperwork and put an end once and for all to a nightmare that had lasted too long. 'That's everything there is . . . Help yourselves.' Because *that* was exactly what there was: papers, boxes, old clothes. They were things that would probably be useless to anyone who wasn't us: forgotten photograph albums; files full of correspondence; documents we might need one day; and, in among all the *papers*, unexpectedly, there were the title deeds to a cemetery plot in which Mum and our grandparents are buried. The family plot. This was the latest snub, which sent us back to that distant day when certain photographs were yanked out of their frames and piled up any old how on the shelves in an office. But this time none of us bothered to ask, 'Why didn't she let us know? It wouldn't have cost her anything.' Neither would we bring to the table long-winded explanations about a fictitious rose bed or the amazing care, according to the one and only version, our father constantly gave the rosebushes. 'Bloody liar' was the heartfelt compliment we paid her. And it was the only one. We stopped there. Let no one think of calling her 'sick', let alone 'mad'. You feel sorry for sick people, and you forgive mad people in the end. There was nothing further from our minds than feeling sorry for her and nothing more ridiculous than to think, even for a few seconds, of forgiving her. Forgetting all about her, that was another thing. Forgetting about her as soon as possible, wherever she was. Whether she was constantly travelling, going back to where she came from or setting up in some other country to cause more havoc. We condemned her to obscurity, to the most complete silence, as if she were dead and buried. We managed to do it, too. We managed it for six and a half years. A little bit of everything happened during those years. We fell in love, there were weddings, separations, divorces and more weddings. During those years one of us moved to a different city, another to a different country. They were years during which we never bothered to remember plots and affronts. Nor, from a distance, did we try to discover the reasons for such inexplicable behaviour. Not until this very morning, the first Christmas we have decided to spend together after a long time, has her name been heard. Like a sonic boom. Barbro, at the most unexpected time, has insisted on showing signs of life – or, to be more precise, signs of death.

We don't really know how these things work. We don't know if the door will open to reveal a stretcher with a body covered with a sheet or if we will have to go into a room full of boxes identified by letters or numbers. We've seen it in the films. There are these gigantic drawers the attendants pull out in front of members of the family or friends who say 'yes' or 'no'. Sometimes they also scream or faint. If we are allowed a choice we would prefer them to bring the body here – although 'prefer' really isn't the right word. We don't prefer anything. But of the two options we think the second one is worse: a whole archive of dead people, perfectly classified and numbered and bitterly cold. Even in the cinema the cold emanates from the screen and freezes the audience.

Neither do we know exactly what happened. Perhaps they'll tell us or perhaps they won't. The only thing we do know is that there is a body and it could be Barbro and that we are here for two possible outcomes: either to identify her positively or to state that we don't recognize the body. The fact that they need us here means that they're not sure, we think. They're not sure about one possibility or the other. They weren't very clear on the telephone this morning. There had been a multiple accident, a mix-up of documents and it was absolutely essential that we came here this afternoon. They didn't use the word 'morgue' but rather 'Institute of Forensic Medicine'. They've taken us so much by surprise that we haven't been able to ask about certain points that are intriguing us now. The first is how they have found us so quickly and the second is what happens in a routine identification. Will they let us stay together all the time, or will we have to go through the ordeal separately? These details are probably not in the least bit important. We are here, and that's all that counts. If we are here it is down to her. It is because of Barbro, because of the woman we'd naïvely buried in our memories.

But, as we are seeing now, the memory isn't a high-security tomb. Merely mentioning her name has unearthed images that are more graphic than ever. And, once again, we've begun to feel angry, indignant and powerless. We thought we'd left these emotions behind, and it's only now that we're able to find the explanation for them that escaped us at the time. Barbro never committed a crime against us that was punishable by law. But she did ridicule the person we loved more than anyone; she invaded our territory; she stole our best memories; she made fun of everything we respected; and she treated us with utter contempt. And now – a leopard can't change its spots – she's reappeared at the most unexpected time, and she's not prepared to spare us a single thing. Not even the final thing – her corpse.

The word 'corpse' sounds strange within these four walls. It sounds strange because it sounds familiar. Here, there are only mortal remains, lifeless bodies with no histories, waiting for an employee to pull open the drawers to show them to the visitors, and then, with a bit of luck, perhaps they can recover their lost individuality. The awful moment, the posthumous gift from the woman our father called Love, still hasn't come around, her final wishes – the pleasure of spoiling things from beyond the grave. We suddenly exchange glances, and there's a flash in our eyes. We don't say a word and can only smile. We know what this means. That flash is an old friend. The first time it appeared, a long time ago, was in the bar on the corner where we used to go every day to drown our sorrows and thrash out ideas. And just like back then, like the day we ended up brandishing the title deeds to a home taken by assault, that flash is telling us 'Danger! Wipe that thought from your minds! Forget about it!' But we're too quick. We understand each other almost without saying a word. We don't need words to understand that this time Barbro (whether the body is hers or not) won't get her own way or that we won't have to go through a rough time. It all seems so simple now. How reassuring. We must have realized it before we even came into this room where we've been waiting for the best part of an hour. We realized it without realizing that we realized it. That happens a lot. That's why as soon as we arrived we invoked scenes from the past – or, rather, certain moments suddenly took root in our minds to show us which path to follow. And here is the path. It's sharp and clear. We don't care about anything else. What happens to the bodies that no one can identify? Are they buried in a common grave? Or is that now outdated and they are given a pauper's funeral as in many other countries? A grave with no inscription? A modest burial niche with a blank tombstone in some sunny cemetery . . . in the South?

We've already mentioned that we don't know how these things work, and neither do we care too much. The fact is that we're not thinking about our Mum and her sweet memory nor about our previous wish for justice – or at least an apology. We're not even thinking about our father. We're simply thinking about ourselves. And about her. For the first time ever she and the three of us seem quite similar. Who would have thought it? Technically, no one can accuse her of having committed any crime. And, for our part, no one will be able to claim we have lied. Because we will not lie. We will not need to falsify anything. We'll be asked if we recognize the body lying on the stretcher, and we'll say 'No'. It will be the plain unvarnished truth. It doesn't much matter which of us three it was who one summer's day discovered the skill that we quickly turned into an art. We'll be here without really being here once again. We'll look without seeing. And now, as the door with the 'NO ENTRY' sign finally begins to open, we get up and don't say a word. But we're already looking with unseeing eyes, and repeating the same words silently to ourselves 'dead cat, dead cat, dead cat'.

A Fresh Start

She had decided to make a fresh start. She had to make a fresh start. And as soon as she arrived at the small apartment-hotel, chosen at random and booked in Barcelona through a travel agent, she thought it was the ideal place to allow her to stop wondering 'How do I go about it?', 'Where do I begin?', 'What's the recipe for starting a new life?' The room was large and bright. There was a kitchenette, a big bed and the bathroom had everything she needed. There was a sofa, armchairs, a dressing-table attached to the wall and a large window looking out on to Gran Vía. The fact that there hadn't been a single room available for these particular dates at her usual hotel in the Paseo del Prado, the one she always went to, had been a stroke of luck. The same thing had happened with all the other alternatives she resorted to whenever her usual hotel told her on the telephone, 'I'm very sorry. We're full up.' Something had to be going on in Madrid during those first few days of spring – a particularly important conference, trade fair or symposium. Now she was glued to the window, protecting her eyes from the sun behind dark glasses and watching the activity in the street, fascinated. It was as if she were watching a silent film with a huge budget. There were thousands of extras, all the colours of the rainbow and lots of action. Some of the actors were trying to attract more attention and play a bigger role.

She had seen one stylish passer-by cross the road at least four or five times. Where on earth was that man going – if indeed he was going anywhere? She moved away from the window and opened her suitcase. Two nights. She would be there only for two nights. But perhaps she would stay longer another time, for a week or a month. She turned on the television and put on the music channel. Then she switched on the air conditioning. For a minute she thought this really was her usual hotel and felt a hankering for what she had lost a long time ago – the urge to read, write, turn the dressing-table into a writing-desk, cook, stock up the fridge, go to the theatre and the cinema. More than anything, she wanted to come back. She wanted to come back to that bright room every evening, and, given the choice, she wouldn't change a thing. It was hers. She had been given a room that belonged to her.

She looked at the key. Room 404. She had liked the number straight away. Four plus four equals eight. The symbol for infinity, she remembered, is a figure 8 on its side. An isolated zero, she thought, in principle has no value. It's nothing. Or perhaps it is something. Perhaps it's not a number but actually a letter. An O for oxygen, for example. She took a deep breath and turned off the television, the music channel and the air conditioning. Then her mind went back to the figure 8, to the key she was still holding in her hand. Four plus four equals eight. Eight months had already passed since *he* had gone. Eight months that time hadn't measured in the usual way. Sometimes those eight months seemed like an eternity, just like the figure 8 on its side. And sometimes they simply seemed like smoke-rings jauntily colliding in the air between puffs on a cigarette. That's what her eight months had been like – interminable and empty.

She went out, and now she was part of the film, too. She was one more extra, one among many thousands. Perhaps at that very moment someone from a double-glazed window, from a sound-proofed room in some hotel, was watching her among the crowd. She liked the thought that whoever was watching her – whether it was a man or a woman – would suddenly feel strangely relaxed and happy, just like she did now. She walked down Gran Vía and thought how lucky she was – the room, such a beautiful day, wanting to get down to work again, to start living again. She had barely walked a block when she stopped in a square. She was surprised that what she thought was a square actually had a street name, calle de la Flor Baja. But that morning wasn't like any other. She'd decided that it wouldn't be like any other. She sat down at a table outside a bar, opened her diary and wrote 'Flor Baja'.

She ordered a beer. She was sure she would never go back to the old hotel in Paseo del Prado. 'Flor Baja' could very well be the starting point for a new itinerary. She would have new interests, start new habits, and perhaps her new life was beginning just at that very moment. She looked through her diary. She had arranged to have dinner with a friend that evening and had to go to an office to sort out some paperwork the next day. Suddenly the very idea of the dinner felt like torture, and it seemed as if the paperwork had just been a pretext to spend a few days in Madrid and have a change of atmosphere. She wrote down, 'Cancel dinner and send documents by post.' She looked at the things she had written down on previous days. There were sayings, suggestions, reminders to be optimistic and how to behave. She smiled as she noticed that in a fit of fury she had ended up striking them all out for being useless. Only two of them had escaped the carnage:

'Live for the day' and Einstein's words of condolence to a friend's widow, 'Your husband has departed this world a little ahead of me, but you know that for me, as a physicist, neither the present nor the past exist.' She couldn't remember the friend's name or his wife's, but she did remember how many times she had read those words in amazement, as if they were meant exclusively for her. The past, the present . . . of course the past existed. The only problem lay in what exactly the past was. Sometimes it insisted on disguising itself as the present. Voices, laughter, whole sentences often made her turn around hopefully in a cinema or in the middle of the street. Just as they would make her toss and turn anxiously when waking up from a dream. But now . . . she called the waiter over and quickly paid for the beer and didn't wait for the change. What was happening now?

She had just seen him. Him. The man who had left this world almost eight months earlier. The man with whom she had shared her whole life. He was wearing an old beige jacket. That beige corduroy jacket! He was absent-mindedly crossing the square in the middle of the calle de la Flor Baja. She followed him cautiously. She was right. Although the similarity was remarkable, she knew it could only be an illusion. But that morning, she'd decided, wasn't like any other. She'd felt that immediately, as soon as she'd walked into room 404 and felt it was hers. It was a morning unlike any other, and he was now walking down Gran Vía, and she was following in his footsteps like a shadow at a sensible distance. A few seconds later he stopped at a news-stand. She saw him hand over a few coins and pick up a packet of cigarettes, and then he moved off again. No, she said to herself, that's not possible. He gave up smoking years ago. Although 'neither the present nor the past exist', she remembered, and it was only then that she thought she understood the reason she'd once written down that sentence to which she repeatedly returned. Perhaps in her new life she would do nothing more than follow any stranger who looked like him. She had no time to feel sorry for herself, to turn around or even to realize that she was behaving like a madwoman. He, whoever he was, had suddenly turned around as if her eyes were burning into the back of his head, and she had no option but to hide in a doorway. She was quick. He didn't see her. But the look on the doorman's face made her realize that she was acting ridiculously. Or was she? She told herself that she wasn't. What was wrong with following someone you love? The man who, defying all the laws of the universe, had reappeared in Madrid in the full light of day one sunny morning delightfully confounding his own past.

She walked into the street again and for the second time in a few minutes felt as if she were taking part in a film, but now she wasn't just another extra, someone to make up the numbers. She was walking surprisingly nimbly, and she had an objective: not to lose sight of the old jacket; to follow it at a distance. And for a few moments she thought that the people walking around and about her realized what she was doing and were aware of her objective. That was why they were looking at her, falling into step with her, spurring her on. But were they really spurring her on? She wasn't young any more and had passed through the doors of invisibility some time ago. She could move around comfortably without anyone paying her any attention. And now, when she needed to be more anonymous and invisible than ever, she was the target of comments, remarks, flirtatious compliments, outrageous proposals. What was happening that morning on Gran Vía? Before she had time to answer her own question he suddenly headed off, taking great strides, and she had to run to keep up with him. She no longer cared that people were looking at her or that some idiot jokingly tried to block her way. She couldn't lose him. Those great strides of his – that was how he walked, with great strides. Then he stopped dead in his tracks. He often used to do that. When he remembered something important he would stop dead in his tracks. She took a deep breath and stopped in front of a perfume shop. Just for a few seconds, she thought, until he moves off again and I can follow him without being noticed. But the glass in a mirror reflected her face back at her, and she just stood there fascinated, astonished and not moving a muscle.

Because it really was her. Who could say how many years ago, but it was her. She was wearing a very short skirt, and her long, shiny chestnut hair was loose. She thought she looked pretty. Very pretty. Had she ever been so pretty? She wanted to think she was in a dream, someone else's dream. Wherever the man she loved was, he was dreaming about her, and now she was looking at herself through his eyes. That's how he must have seen her around the time they met; that time, so long ago now, when anything seemed possible. She took a great big breath and had the feeling she had already experienced that moment. The shop window, the mirror, her girlish reflection, Gran Vía one sunny morning. A mirage or simply an optical illusion. The sun, her reflection, a trick of the mirror, the objects and posters in the window becoming entwined with her own image.

'Where did you get to?' she suddenly heard.

She put her hand out to stop herself from falling over. He was there – tall, slim and just as young as when they first knew each other. There was no longer any doubt. The boy in the beige jacket was right there, behind her, and he'd just put his hand on her shoulder.

'Come on. We're late. Don't forget, we're meeting up with Tete.'

He put his arm around her waist, and she let herself be led away like an automaton. Tete Poch. Tete Poch had died years before. Tete was the first of their friends to disappear, to abandon this world. But now it seemed as if none of this could have happened yet. Tete was still alive. He had not yet departed to the place from which there is no return, and she was a girl with long hair who wore amazingly short skirts. She took a deep breath, and once again thought she might faint. She bit her lip until it bled. It wasn't a dream. This was really happening. She gradually recognized streets, shops and bars. They went into one that seemed surprisingly familiar. She knew the place. There was a time she used to go there regularly, although she couldn't now remember its name. A blotchy mirror reflected back her face. She was still pretty. And there he was beside her, very, very young, wearing that nice corduroy jacket he never wanted to take off and which she still (without knowing why) kept in the wardrobe.

'Tete's borrowed a car off someone. We could go to Segovia for the day.'

'Great.'

'What's up? You've hardly said a thing all morning.'

She shook her head.

'You were walking so quickly . . .'

Tete hadn't arrived yet. It was better that way. She needed some time to take in what was happening. He had just taken out a book from his pocket.

'I found it in an old bookshop yesterday. It's a real gem.'

She looked at the cover. *The Oresteia* by Aeschylus. She was surprised that she could read the title without her glasses. Her sight was still good back then. Perhaps, but anyway she'd recognized the book immediately. It was still at home, too, on the bookshelf in the study. She hadn't dared take anything out of that room, even though he had gone.

'It's a trilingual edition,' he said proudly. 'Classical Greek, Modern Greek and English.'

'Yes.'

He took her hand. 'Something's up with you. Or are you worried about the exam?'

The exam? What exam?

'I'm sure you've passed. Don't worry.'

She suddenly began remembering: Tete, a beaten-up old car, the three of them in Segovia, the journalism exam. That's why they'd gone to Madrid. She had to take an exam in journalism, and *he'd* gone with her. They went everywhere together, almost from the first time they'd met at the Faculty of Law in Barcelona. They were never boyfriend and girlfriend. They didn't like those words. They hated them. They were friends. That's what they used to say. 'FRIENDS' in capital letters. No one had been surprised that some years later the friendship turned into marriage, although they didn't like the word 'marriage' either and 'husband' and 'wife' even less. They thought they sounded formal and boring. If anyone had asked them what they were back then, at the time Tete was around and when they used to go to Madrid and when she was taking the journalism exam, they would have said 'FRIENDS'.

'I'm just going to the toilet,' she said, and he stroked her cheek. Her cheek, my God, her cheek was burning! She was scared she would burst into tears, get emotional, say something out of place and spoil the marvellous encounter. She got up and added, 'I'll be back in a minute.'

She didn't need to ask where the toilets were or stop to look at the sign ('TOILETS. TELEPHONE') because she knew exactly where she was. It was as if she had been there just the day before. She went down a couple of steps and turned back to look at the table. Tete had just arrived, and they were giving each other a hug. They were giving each other a hug! Then she did burst into tears. Tears of joy, tears of forgotten joy. Her mascara had run into one eye, and she almost had to feel her way down to the toilets. She splashed some water on her face when she got there. She needed to clear her head and sort herself out. She had to look happy and carefree and think there was still a whole life ahead of them. If they were surprised at how she looked or guessed that she'd been crying, she would simply say, 'Bloody mascara. I don't know why I bother with make-up.' She suddenly remembered that that was exactly what had happened. She remembered it clearly, word for word. 'Bloody mascara. I don't know why I bother with make-up.' She also clearly remembered that, on that morning she'd miraculously been allowed to relive, her eyes had stung for a long time and they went to a chemist's and bought eye-drops (which brand was it?). Then they all got into the borrowed car and sang songs the whole way. Back then it was quite a journey to get to Segovia. They sang war songs, anthems, banned lyrics that were just as forbidden as the fact that she, a girl of twenty years of age at the time, should be in a car with Tete and him, as free as birds, happy and carefree, while her parents in Barcelona thought she was taking an exam or studying. What a charmed life they'd led before mobile phones. She dried her face with a towel (paper towels still hadn't invaded the toilets) and went up the steps two at a time. She was ready. She knew the script and was happy. She was the happiest girl in the world, even though her mascara was still running and for a moment, when she rubbed her eyes, she could see only a grey mist. Bloody mascara!

For a second she thought she'd made a mistake and that the bar had another room or that the toilets were shared between two different premises. But there was only one staircase and upstairs was a soulless bar with an enormous counter, a few customers and a dozen tables piled up any old how in a corner. 'Where are the young men who were here a short while ago?' she asked a waiter in a quavering voice. The man shrugged and didn't understand. She leaned against the wall. Where had they gone? How could they leave her behind?

A young woman offered her a seat and asked, 'Are you OK?' She shook her head.

'She seems confused,' said the waiter. 'She came in a while ago and went straight to the toilets.'

The young woman spoke to her gently, very slowly and in a loud voice as if she were a foreigner who found it difficult to understand. 'What's your address? Shall we call a taxi for you?'

She didn't reply. She opened her handbag and took out a small mirror and looked at herself in it for a moment. She wasn't surprised. In the distance she could hear a hum of voices wondering what was going on and the young woman asking for a napkin with some ice-cubes and talking to the onlookers.

'It's all right. The lady doesn't feel very well.'

She went back to the hotel, to the apartment-room she had

liked so much that morning. The past, the present, she remembered. There is no past and there is no present. Today, the present had slipped into her past. Or it was the other way around and fragments of her past had surfaced in the present? She opened her suitcase. By this time they would already be on the way to Segovia. Once more she wondered how they could have left her behind. But taking the high-speed train would mean she could overtake them and get there before they did. The present racing against the past. Not everything was lost yet because once again she remembered everything perfectly well: the restaurant, as much wine as you could drink, searching out a cheap hotel for the night. The names and the exact locations didn't matter. She would go to each and every restaurant, inn, tavern or hostelry until she found them. It would be best to leave her suitcase down at reception and travel without any luggage. There wasn't a second to lose. She would take a taxi and go to Chamartín Station. She'd catch up with them and would reappear in that delightful day from so long ago. Tete, him and her, with their whole lives ahead of them.

The key slipped out of her hand and clattered on the floor. She saw the number on the key fob and smiled. She smiled. 'Eight months, oxygen, four plus four, infinity.' She kneeled down, picked up the key and couldn't help recalling her thoughts from just a short while ago, her frustration or despair at her question 'How could they leave me behind?' But also, as she was leaning against the bed to help herself get up, she was grateful for the miracle of time travel, the hope that if *that* (whatever it was) had happened it could happen again; clinging to Einstein's words, which had become a mantra: 'There is no past and there is no present.' Suddenly she understood that she'd made a mistake about something very important. They hadn't left her behind. How could she have thought something so ridiculous? Of course they hadn't left her behind. There they were, the three of them, together on the road in an old banger someone had lent them, singing and laughing. They were free! That day from years and years back she had experienced once again just for a few moments was not over. She squeezed the key as if it were an amulet. 404. Oxygen. Four plus four equals eight. Infinity was a figure 8 on its side. She opened her hand without realizing it; the key slipped from it once more and hit the floor. But now she thought it was mocking her. *A fresh start. A fresh start. A fresh start.*

She sat down at the dressing-table and looked at herself in the mirror. She wouldn't go anywhere. The past had a cast-iron script, and there could be no improvisation. Whatever Einstein said, the past and the present were two irreconcilable spaces. She had been on the verge of doing something crazy; the whole morning had been completely ridiculous. If she closed her eyes she could still see and hear them – the songs, the car and the road – but if she opened her eyes she saw her tired old face again. That's what her new life was offering her. It would be no use to try to cheat the clock and steal back times that didn't belong to her any more. For a moment she saw herself, exhausted and in a sweat, finally finding the bar where the three friends were cheerfully chatting and discreetly sitting down at a nearby table to watch them and to wait for the miracle to work its magic once again. But now she felt ridiculous. She felt like an intruder, an interloper, a gooseberry, because those three were twenty years old; they were young and living for the moment. And, what was now clearer than ever, they didn't need her for anything. They didn't need a sixty-year-old woman staring into a mirror who sometimes, occasionally, didn't feel very well.

A Few Days
with the
Wahyes-Wahno

I had always thought that my aunt and uncle, Valeria and Tristán, were happy and full of fun, but more than anything else they seemed young, really young, although perhaps they were already fifty years old or thereabouts. They were completely different from our parents and our parents' friends. In fact, they were completely different from anyone else. That's why I was extremely surprised that our parents sent my brother and me to stay with them in the mountains for the whole month of August that summer. They said over and over again that we would be able to breathe the pure mountain air, eat fresh eggs and drink goat's milk straight from the goat. But the real surprise wasn't the pure mountain air, the milk or the eggs. It was them. Just them. They were the bizarre, foolish, lackadaisical couple; the happy-go-lucky couple. Out of all the terms our family regularly used to describe their lifestyle the one I liked the best and the one that at the same time intrigued me most was 'happy-go-lucky'. I imagined them in the privacy of their home, in the dining-room, the kitchen, the bedroom, taking bundles of clothes, sheets, tablecloths, throwing them up into the air and letting them fall back down shouting 'Go with the flow!' – the catchphrase of theirs that seemed to encapsulate their happy-go-lucky approach to life. They had an even better time with the pots and pans. Not to mention dancing in the dining-room to music from an old gramophone, waiting for the record to play the last few notes then throwing it up to the ceiling, celebrating when it came back down and stamping on it with delight, with a few signature chants of 'Go with the flow!' thrown in for good measure. I thought this routine could almost have been borrowed from the Frank Capra film my mother always talked about, *You Can't Take It with You*. Although I had not yet seen it back then, I could quote some scenes almost word for word. Thinking back, it seems strange now that my mother was so fascinated by that black-and-white celluloid home where there were no obligations or rules. It was happy-go-lucky, just like her brother's and sister-in-law's house. Because I wasn't wrong about that. There was complete freedom in Uncle Tristán's and Aunt Valeria's house. Compared with theirs, any other home seemed like a prison or a zoo. That's why we were delighted. Surprised but delighted. And at that time we didn't even know anything about the Wahyes-Wahno.

My aunt and uncle didn't have children because they hadn't wanted any. There was much talk about that in the family. Some people said they were selfish. Others – and my mother was one of those – thought it was better that way, as small defenceless children wouldn't fit into their lifestyle. As for their lifestyle, I never got any clear information about it. They travelled a lot. They were always studying, reading, writing and painting. But was that a bad thing? No one definitively told me that it was, although anyone I asked generally shrugged, shook their heads with a smile or, best of all, with a certain air of superiority came out with words such as 'artists', 'bohemians', 'lazybones', 'feckless' and, of course, 'happy-go-lucky'. Aunt Berta, my father's sister, loved criticizing them more than anyone. But Aunt Berta thought she was perfect. She liked interfering, wouldn't accept any way of life other than her own and came down heavily on anyone who dared to contradict her. I hated her, and she knew it. I hated her with good reason, as she had destroyed my Human Races scrapbook with all my drawings and comments. 'This is madness,' she had declared that day to my complete bewilderment. 'You'll have to go to the doctor's.' She was like that. If it were down to her, she would have sent us all to see a psychiatrist at the slightest excuse. But all that had happened at least three years earlier when we had a miserable time staying at her house at the beach. I was ten years old then, almost eleven. It was summertime, too, just like now. Today, however, we were happy on the coach, feeling the strange sensation of the pressure change blocking our ears as we climbed; our faces glued to the windows watching rivers with clear blue water, pine forests, stone houses with slate roofs go past. We had seen all this before only on postcards or in magazines. When we got to the last village on the route we saw our aunt and uncle sitting outside the bar in the square. They ran over, helped us down and took charge of our suitcases. I think even then they said 'Wahyes, Wahyes' when they greeted us. But my brother and I were so happy that neither of us noticed.

Outside, everything smelled of manure, chickens and goats, just like we'd been told it would, but inside the house it didn't. As soon as we went in I caught my brother with his nose in the air, sniffing like a bloodhound. I didn't tell him off because I was doing exactly the same, albeit more discreetly. There was a strong smell. I couldn't say whether it was pleasant or quite the opposite. It was a mixture of paint, cake, chocolate, wine, perfume and perhaps incense like you get in a church. I would find out later that one of Valeria's hobbies was creating different scents and that some came out well and others were not so successful. But that day, when I still knew hardly anything at all, what I noticed more than anything was the kitchen. It was enormous and full of pipes and test-tubes, just like the kind of magician's laboratory you see in films. And we liked it. We both did. It was all very different from what we'd known up to then. Beginning with them, our aunt and uncle. It was the first time we had been on our own with them without being under the watchful gaze of the rest of the family, and the long summer that stretched ahead of us seemed filled with promise. They put us in the same room. It was an enormous bedroom, and while Valeria was handing out sheets and towels Tristán asked me discreetly, 'How's your father? Is he any better?'

I shook my head. He was ill, seriously ill and needed peace and quiet. That was why the dining-room at home had been turned into his bedroom, and it was also why they'd decided that the best thing for everyone would be for Pedrito and me to spend the month of August with them.

'Why not Berta's house?' My uncle didn't beat around the bush, and I liked that, too. He was frank and direct, and he was surprised, just like us. I shrugged.

'Mum said that pure mountain air, fresh eggs, goat's milk . . .'

Tristán began to roar with laughter, which made him seem even younger. Perhaps that's why I started telling him about my differences with Aunt Berta, how much I hated her. Because I'd never forgotten that morning in her house overlooking the sea when I'd decided not to go to the beach and had stayed in the garden inventing different races. It hadn't occurred to me that this might be a bad thing to do. And I was still sure that it wasn't. So I looked at Tristán and began at the beginning.

I told him that a school friend had a scrapbook and that every week she put new stickers in it. They were coloured stickers that showed men and women from far-off places, with gigantic earrings in their ears or rings in their noses or lips. There were black people, brown people, yellow people and white people, too. Some of them wore their hair in plaits, while others had hair that was all tousled and a few had shaved their heads, some just a bit and others completely. Their very different and very strange customs were explained in comments beneath the stickers and sometimes along the side. I wanted a collection like that as well, but the people who ran the village stationer's didn't know anything about scrapbooks or stickers – or at least not those ones. So I decided to make my own. I bought card, paper, crayons and started my own collection: Human Races. I spent the whole morning working at it. I invented people, tribes, names and, in particular, customs, very strange customs like the ones in my friend's scrapbook. That's what I was doing when Aunt Berta appeared.

Tristán looked interested as he was listening to me, and I carried on telling him how at first Aunt Berta was just looking over my shoulder to see what I was doing. Just at first. I was getting angrier and angrier as I was recalling it all. But now, years afterwards, as I rekindle the memory, I'm grateful rather than angry. Because if Aunt Berta hadn't crumpled up and spoiled my scrapbook, if she hadn't told me off as she did talking about doctors and crazy games, I wouldn't have told Tristán anything about my collection of races. And probably he would never have decided to let us into his secret world. All he said back then was 'A natural anthropologist.'

I detected a hint of pride in his voice and tried to remember exactly what 'anthropologist' meant. I thought I knew, but I wasn't sure.

'And your Aunt Berta wouldn't have liked that at all,' he said a little while later rather mysteriously.

That night, after dinner, Valeria asked Pedrito if he'd like a glass of milk. To my surprise he said yes enthusiastically. But Valeria didn't disappear in search of a goat to milk in front of him as my brother was clearly expecting. Instead, she opened the fridge and handed him an ordinary carton very similar to the ones we had at home. Then, not even noticing his disappointment, she tied up her long dark hair in a plait, adjusted her apron, forgot all about us and began dissolving some powder in a salad bowl and crushing herbs in a pestle and mortar. Almost at the same time Tristán cleared the table, unfolded an enormous map and pinned the edges down with whatever he could find in the cupboard: an old iron, a broken jar, a stone and an earthenware teapot. My brother and I looked at each other in confusion. Should we say goodnight and go to bed? Could we stay with them in the kitchen a little longer? The situation was new for us, and I understand now that it wasn't too clear for them either. They weren't used to dealing with kids or teenagers. Perhaps, for them, nine-year-old Pedrito and me, at almost fourteen, were exactly the same. But if they were ever in any doubt they quickly got over it, and, apart from the glass of milk for my brother every night that my mother must have insisted on, they treated us as equals, as adults or friends, which had never happened to either of us before.

'Well,' said Tristán once he had the map securely pinned down, 'have you ever heard of the Wahyes-Wahno?'

We shook our heads but realized that we were being invited to take part in the event of the evening.

'I'm not surprised. In fact, if you'd said yes I wouldn't have believed you. But let's begin at the beginning so that we all know where we are. As you know, I'm your uncle, your much-loved mother's only brother, and the incomparable Valeria is my wife.' Valeria acknowledged this with a nod but didn't take her eyes off the mortar. 'And I'm an anthropologist, apart from being an expert in many other fields that are not relevant here but of which you may be aware: an artist, a lazybones, a bohemian and a feckless fool.'

'Go with the flow!' shouted Pedrito enthusiastically, and for all I was worth I wanted the ground to swallow me up.

'That as well. How could I forget? Thanks for reminding me, Pedrito. That's a good name for our house. "Go with the flow!" What do you think, Valeria?'

Valeria smiled and nodded. She was completely absorbed in her work with the pestle and mortar, as if it were the most important thing in the world. She had got into a regular rhythm that was almost musical. It was like an accompaniment that slightly muffled what Tristán was saying but which now, during these pauses, took on its own unexpected role. It was nice to listen to and lose yourself in its music as the kitchen began to fill up with an aroma of earth, grass, leaves and meadows after rain. There was another smell, too, that I couldn't quite place, but it seemed to me that it was struggling to make its presence felt and to spiral up among all the other aromas. To overcome them.

'Let's get back to where we were.' It was Tristán's voice again, and Valeria's music faded into the background. 'As we're among friends and not at a conference or in court, I'll spare you the preliminaries. But just so you know, although it's not strictly necessary, it's common practice these days before presenting a hypothesis to spend a few minutes annihilating all the other hypotheses bearing the slightest resemblance to one's own that any colleague might have dared to touch upon.'

He looked at me as if he were talking to an equal. As if I were a future anthropologist. So I nodded like I understood. I couldn't disappoint him.

'All I will say is that, in principle, we should not give the slightest credence to any hypothetical study about the Wahyes-Wahno or to the alleged photographs taken with powerful zoom lenses or to the news of sightings of their settlements at inconceivable distances. We are all aware of this. It's easy to confuse wishful thinking with reality.'

He stopped, and the rhythm of Valeria's pestle and mortar and the smell of damp earth took over the kitchen once again. Tristán was tracing the vast areas of green on the map with his index finger and murmuring wistfully 'Amazonia, Amazonia'. I watched him closely, not worrying whether my ignorance would show on my face or bothering to pretend to understand. I was completely absorbed in the massive area spread out in front of me on the table. Suddenly, as if I were looking at it through a powerful magnifying glass, it took on every conceivable shade of green: olive, emerald, turquoise, mint and lime. And then, as if I were beginning to dream or beginning, delightfully and drowsily, to fall asleep, Tristán's voice took possession of my body. There was nothing else in the kitchen apart from his voice, strong and measured.

'Wishful thinking and reality,' he said again. 'It's so easy to confuse them. It's even easier to confuse them in the jungle in the tropics when you're in the grip of drowsiness, feverish sleepiness or those disturbing dreams you often get in those places when the past, the present and the future merge into one and which seem so real and confuse us so much that when we wake up we usually take hours or even days to realize and accept who we are. Because as long as the dream lasts', he continued looking at me straight in the eyes, 'people could turn into their own parents or their own children or into indigenous people like the Cashibo-Kakataibo, the Yanomami or the Awá, to give you some examples. They could also speak, sing and whistle in the language of the Pirahas. What's even more amazing is that they could listen to and remember the final words of the last Pacahuara in the world.' Tristán stopped there, and I took a deep breath as well. I could not remember ever having paid so much attention to anyone before.

'That's one of the loveliest dreams. It's a privilege and a great honour for any one of us. The Pacahuara lying on his rush mat is looking at us, full of emotion. He knows he's about to die and that there's no cure to keep him alive. He also knows that on his death his language, or the little he remembers of what his language once was, will disappear. His language was corrupted in the first place by other more powerful people then forgotten as he was the last of his kind and had no one to talk to. But at that awful moment, on his deathbed, if the Pacahuara is a man, he remembers his parents and grandparents; the stories he was told as a child; his first bow and arrow; the silvery reflections of the fish he used to catch with a spear in those far-off days. Or, if the Pacahuara is a woman, she remembers washing clothes in the river; the songs she used to sing as she crushed sweet potatoes in a bowl; the pain of childbirth; the names of people who had disappeared; the times when she wasn't alone and she could still use and listen to words that after being forgotten for years were now suddenly and vividly returning to her mind. Because that's what the last Pacahuara dreams about, irrespective of whether he is a man or she is a woman. Past memories are recovered, and recent memories are wiped away. He points at whoever he's dreaming about, takes him by the hand and, making an enormous effort, tells him his final words, which will also be, as both he and the person he's talking to are aware, the last words ever spoken in his language.'

As he was talking I was filling that vast green territory with the people he was describing. And I could feel what they were feeling. The emotion of an anthropologist, explorer or traveller who at that time knows he is unique. He hasn't understood a single word of what the dying person has said, whether he's just expressed his last wishes, made a pronouncement or merely uttered some downright nonsense or some words that don't make the least bit of sense. But he's now received a message that no one will ever be able to decipher, and he's the sole protagonist of a historic moment. The sound of the dying man's words will accompany him for days and days (and he will constantly repeat them so as not to forget them) until another anthropologist, explorer or traveller tells him he had a similar meeting. The last words of the last Pacahuara, whether a man or a woman. The precious legacy of a dead language. The unforgettable cadence of those mysterious words that he has been able to retain in his mind to pass on to posterity. And that's where everything begins to unravel. What the second anthropologist, explorer or traveller remembers by heart and is ready to communicate, bursting with emotion, is nothing like the words, sound and cadence that the first anthropologist, explorer or traveller has chiselled into his brain.

'And after that portentous moment,' concluded Tristán, 'without any need for words both of them will understand: it's all down to the drowsiness induced by the climate; wish-fulfilment; tricks that the jungle plays; dreams.'

Pedrito nodded off on the table, and almost at the same time the glass mortar that Valeria was using exploded and fell on the floor. Or perhaps it fell on the floor first and then exploded into thousands of pieces. What's certain is that a strong whiff took over the kitchen. I recognized the smell of grass, rain, damp ground, leaves, but I also detected the emanation that was struggling against the rest and that had finally won. Now I knew what it reminded me of: stagnant water, rotten fruit, mouldy food. I thought something awful was about to happen, that Tristán would get cross with his wife or that Valeria would apologize profusely for the disaster. I was silly to think like that, but I was remembering the commotion at home when Pedrito spilled a glass of water on the table or got drops of sauce or soup on the tablecloth. But my aunt's and uncle's life was nothing like ours. Tristán was really pleased, even thrilled, and Valeria, still smiling, squatted down to separate all the pieces of glass carefully so that she could recover the strong smelling paste and put it in a test-tube.

'You've really nailed it today!' said Tristán. 'If I close my eyes I can imagine I'm still there.'

Valeria rubbed a bit of the paste on her temples and also on her wrists. She was radiant. I kneeled down and wrapped up a few lumps in a paper napkin.

'How fantastic!' said Tristán.

When I got to our room I wrote down some names in a notebook so that I wouldn't forget them: Yanomami; Awá; Pacahuara; Wahyes-Wahno. I put a line under Pacahuara as they'd been the evening's protagonists and put a question mark beside Wahyes-

Wahno, as all I knew about them was that no one knew anything about them. Pedrito was sleeping deeply, and I could hear laughter and the odd word, which soon turned into murmurs and moans coming from my aunt's and uncle's room. I had seen lots of films and was old enough to understand what was going on. I covered my ears with a handkerchief and smeared the little bit of paste I had in the napkin on my forehead. It smelled awful, but I wanted to be like my aunt and uncle. I'd get used to it. If they liked that smell, then I would, too.

My aunt and uncle always wandered around the house barefoot and did their exercises naked every morning. Then they got dressed for breakfast. I thought they got dressed because of us, so that Pedrito wouldn't think of telling Mum and she wouldn't regret having sent us to stay with her brother. Mum phoned every evening before dinner. Tristán would tell her that everything was fine and would ask her 'Any news from the palace?' It was his way of finding out how Dad was without upsetting us. Then he sent her lots of love and handed the phone over to us. I would say, 'Everything's fine', and Pedrito would tell her all sorts of things: that he always drank his glass of milk; that he had swum in a very cold river; or that when he grew up he wanted to be a savage. Then Mum would burst out laughing and everyone was happy.

The telephone was the only way to communicate with the world we had left behind. It was almost an antique and was positioned exactly halfway down the corridor, and when someone phoned you could hear their voice anywhere in the house as if the radio was on. But we didn't have a radio. My aunt and uncle liked listening to the wind, the rain, the cicadas, the neighbours' hens or the goats bleating as they came down the mountain every evening.

Sometimes Valeria used to sing, and she sang beautifully. She sang songs without any words – at least without any words that I could understand. She shouted, laughed, and it sometimes sounded as if she were crying. Tristán told us very quietly that she'd once been an actress and that she sometimes liked to remind herself of that. I would have liked to have asked her about lots of things – her life as an actress, for example, or their travels or where and when they'd met – but I didn't want them to think I was being too inquisitive, so I kept quiet. I don't know if I did the right thing. I still wonder about that years later. What's true is that many of the things that perplexed me at the time became clear all on their own. The supermarket, for example. At the beginning I thought it was strange that my aunt and uncle, who loved the pure mountain air, rivers, goats and hens, in short, nature itself, didn't buy their eggs, cheese or milk from their neighbours in the village and instead once a week got their van out of the garage and drove for at least twenty kilometres to a larger village that had a supermarket. Perhaps the products were almost as good, I thought at first. They were from the same region after all. Then I understood that my aunt and uncle simply wanted to keep their distance from the other people in their village. They certainly greeted everyone, and we sometimes went to the only bar in the square to have something to drink and wait for the last coach of the day. Just like all the other villagers, we liked counting the number of passengers arriving and the number of passengers leaving, making predictions, placing bets and arguing with the other tables about the possible rules of the game. Was a baby worth the same as an adult? How much was a cage of hens worth? The same as a dog or less? And how come there had never been a draw? There was even one afternoon when Tristán delightedly took the place of a domino player and won a few games. But while we were there no one from the village ever came to the house or came to visit us for any reason. There was clearly something about our aunt's and uncle's behaviour that made everyone else respect their privacy. They were friendly, polite and kind, but it went no further than that. Pedrito and I were aware of it and felt that we were privileged. Just like the last Pacahuara from the first night – more to the point, just like the anthropologist, explorer or traveller who was honoured or lucky enough to dream about the Pacahuara's last words in the jungle.

That's why, on our second night after dinner, I plucked up the courage to remind them, 'We were talking about the last Pacahuara, about the dreams.'

I had pronounced 'Pacahuara' as if I were used to it and without stumbling, certain that they would be proud of my memory and diction. But Tristán didn't seem astonished in the slightest. Valeria wasn't either. A few minutes later, however, my uncle once again unfolded the map awash with shades of green and Valeria began crushing garlic and seeds in a stone mortar. 'The music will be very different today,' she said.

She was right. But it wasn't only the rhythm that was different. It was also Tristán's words, his intonation and, above all, his urgency. He was strangely anxious to finish one subject as soon as possible and get on to another. He polished off the Pacahuara in four rushed sentences and did the same with the dreams. It had only been an introduction, he told us, a way of making us understand how deceptive the jungle can be and to appreciate the dangers lying in wait for anyone entering its depths. And, as if he were closing a chapter with that and had nothing else to add, he filled his pipe, nodded his head in time to Valeria's rhythm and just like the other night traced his finger over the green expanse of Amazonia. I guessed that he was getting ready to talk about what he was really interested in, and I waited in silence.

'Do you want to know how I met the Wahyes-Wahno?' he suddenly asked.

Pedrito opened up his drawing book and tried out a few crayons. It was better that way. If he kept himself amused he wouldn't fall asleep. I nodded. 'The Wahyes-Wahno,' I said softly.

'All right then,' said Tristán, and I thought I could see a glint of something I didn't recognize in his eyes. 'It was a few years back, twenty years ago maybe. I had got lost in the middle of the jungle. What's more, I had lost all notion of time and there was no possibility of contacting the others in the expedition. I was alone, exhausted and injured.'

I immediately imagined him bare-chested with his trousers in tatters, wearing a cartridge belt and a rifle slung over one shoulder. I wondered if pith helmets were worn in the Amazon as they were in Africa in the films. But the question never even left my head. Definitely not, I thought, answering myself. The trees must be so tall that no sun would filter through, and, even if he had worn one at the beginning, with all the danger and exhaustion it would probably have fallen off some time ago. So I gave him a red bandanna tied around his head instead. That was the only time I stopped listening. It was the only time I let my thoughts wander from his story for even a few seconds. And once again, just like the previous day, his powerful voice worked its magic. It was as if the map spread out on the table was soaking up all the light in the kitchen and as if nothing else existed apart from the festival of green that was gradually opening up like theatre curtains. Tristán was talking, and, going into the depths of the jungle, I could see him there, with his clothes in tatters and the red bandanna tied around his head covering a small wound. He was insignificant in the face of such immensity and about to be swallowed up by the vegetation. Until suddenly I lost this picture of him in my head and I felt I was in the middle of a circle going around faster and faster and there was no way out. There was no more olive, emerald, turquoise, mint and lime. There was just green. It was a green with no differentiating shades that was threatening to devour me at any moment. Then I understood that far from having lost my uncle I was *seeing everything through his eyes* and that at any second Tristán, the exhausted, battered and injured Tristán in the jungle, would faint and fall to the ground flat on his face. I closed my eyes to escape from the green tornado and to save him as well. But I opened them almost straight away. Now my uncle was roaring with laughter.

'I lost consciousness. I fainted, or perhaps I died. I'll never know. But when I came to I thought I'd been the victim of one of those jungle dreams I was talking to you about yesterday in which the past, future and present all become confused.'

The first thing Tristán saw when he opened his eyes was a woman from an ethnic group he didn't recognize staring at him. She was very short and almost naked, and there were strange markings on her face that he thought were geometric shapes he'd never seen before. She was carrying two very young babies in a kind of sling around her neck. One of them was on her back and the other against her breast. She bent her head down, and her lips didn't move. But he understood what she was thinking. He understood that she was welcoming him and said to himself, I'm dreaming. I've fallen into one of those jungle traps. The fact is that seeing the mother and her two babies gave him such a feeling of comforting peace that he wasn't able to explain it even now. It was as if he'd known her from way back or as if he'd been waiting for her for years and years without even realizing it. Perhaps because of all that, because of the emotion and also his dreadful state, he collapsed yet again. He took a deep breath and lost consciousness once more. 'Or died again. Who knows?' he said lighting his pipe. And to my surprise he burst out laughing again. 'Sometimes life is amazingly magnanimous,' he eventually continued, and the glint in his eyes was even brighter. 'You may be seeking a single jewel, and, when you least expect it, you come across a whole hoard!'

He stopped for a bit, and all we could hear was Valeria's beating and bashing. Then, still smiling, he looked back at us and continued.

'Our expedition had other objectives, and it doesn't matter now what they were. But, lost in the thick of the jungle, I was rescued by a Wahyes-Wahno, and she introduced me to the secrets of her tribe.'

Because back then even less was known about the Wahyes-Wahno than the little that's known today: just their name, fleeting and unconnected pieces of news about them, mostly gleaned from explorers' fantasies or from recurring dreams that the victims clung to when they woke up. So at the beginning Tristán could name neither his rescuer nor the tribe that welcomed him back to consciousness after he had collapsed the second time. He simply came to, and this time he saw about a dozen men and women bent over him, staring at him in amazement. They didn't look hostile. And they weren't. But, as he would soon find out, they knew how to defend themselves, take their revenge for insults and, most notably, melt into their environment and become almost invisible. Their mimicry and natural talent for camouflage was their main defensive weapon. That's why they'd hardly ever been seen, and, even if they were caught out, they managed to slip away like eels, climbing up to the tops of the trees or scattering in all directions. For many people they were nothing more than a myth. They didn't exist other than in legend, the irrational fear of different tribes or in the confused stories told by loggers, those ruthless, brutish and cruel men, destroyers of the jungle and hated by all the tribes, who make relentless advances in deforestation but who are at the same time seized by panic when attacked by the Wahyes-Wahno and are unable to fight against an enemy that never shows itself. Arrows flew out of the thick of the jungle as if they were shot by the very trees the invaders were trying to chop down – an ipe or lapacho or any other species of tree. It would be said (and more than one logger, so the story goes, would end up losing his mind) that the whole plant kingdom had united to protect itself. But it would also be said that the iron will and power of a people was behind this organized vengeance and that was why the arrows broke the silence whistling *wahyessss-wahnoooo*. That, at least, was what was said in the sawmills and among the loggers.

'And I won't say it wasn't so.' Now Tristán was very carefully rolling up the map as if our session were coming to an end. 'It's possible that my friends put their names to their arrows, but I can only talk about their attacks at one remove. I was never frightened, and long before their lips moved I knew I was safe.'

So, in the same way that the woman had said 'Welcome' to him without using any words, now the whole tribe made him aware of their very best intentions and welcomed him into the tribe as one more member, urging him to keep their existence secret, as if it were their most precious gift. And he felt the words that no one spoke within his whole being, as if they were a part of his own thoughts or as if he were still suffering the effects of his collapse. But nothing could have been further from the truth. Because at one point, and always simply using his mind, he thanked the tribe for their kindness and care, and when he did so he felt an electric current flowing from his mind and lighting up the foreheads of his benefactors. And vice versa. When they were revealing their ancestral history to him, repeating that he had nothing to fear, or when they were explaining to him the properties of certain plants they'd begun using to treat his injuries, he felt an invisible force, an energy emitted by the Wahyes-Wahno that entered his mind and stimulated conversation. As he would soon discover, this was one of their many forms of communication, and they frequently made use of it, for example, when danger loomed, when members of the tribe were scattered and also (although only very exceptionally) when they wanted to mix with people who, like Tristán, didn't know their language. Because their language was beautiful, musical and complex. The spoken word and silence were both accorded equal value. Until then Tristán had never known a people who held silence in such high esteem and who also fully appreciated the value of the spoken word.

'And the first word I heard from their lips', he continued, 'was *Wahyessss*, stretched out with all the stress on the final syllable. One man began, a woman joined in, followed by the whole tribe.'

Tristán – as he would soon tell us – quickly realized that these people had named themselves or used the first part of the name by which they were known. But it was only later, when he had already spent a few days in their village and his injuries had almost healed, that he understood what it really meant. *Wahyes* implied acceptance, welcome, a YES in capital letters; *Wahno* implied the opposite. He only witnessed the terrifying *Wahnooooo* on one occasion, when it was aimed at someone from another tribe who had approached the village alone and, according to my uncle, whose only intention was to parley, to ask for information, to propose a truce or perhaps let them know about imminent danger. But the Wahyes-Wahno didn't see it like that, and our uncle had no option but to admit his mistake. So, *Wahnooooo* was etched on the atmosphere as a warning, an accusing finger, the archangel's flaming sword banishing our forefathers from Paradise. There is no exact translation for it in any language, and 'get lost', 'go away', 'we don't like you', 'get out of here', 'enough' would be weak and incomplete equivalents with no power at all. *Wahnooooo* expressed total rejection. It was like a shot going in through your ears and boring into your soul.

Tristán stopped talking and looked thoughtful, and no one dared break his silence. For a few seconds all you could hear was Valeria's rhythmic pounding of that night's earthy aromatic concoction, and I felt as though the smell of garlic was becoming even stronger and was threatening to take over the kitchen and suffocate us.

'And, now, off to bed,' said Tristán, suddenly tired. 'That's enough, Valeria. It hasn't worked today.'

Valeria shrugged her shoulders. She gave us both a kiss, stroked my brother's head and emptied out the mortar into the rubbish.

From then on we wouldn't have to wait until night-time to return to the jungle. The next morning, down beside the river, Valeria started weaving branches and leaves in the style of the Wahyes-Wahno and showed us how to slide into the water on tiptoe, slipping gently in from among the trees. Slide in, she insisted, never jump or throw yourself in. The idea was to do as they did and give the river time to open its doors without breaking into it, surprising it or waking it abruptly from its slumber. Sometimes I thought that nothing I saw could be true, such as watching her climb a tree, grasping the branches and, as supple as a leopard, diving off, flying through the air and majestically entering the water. She wasn't wearing a swimming costume, just a cotton wrap around her body. Perhaps that's why we used to swim in a pool a fair distance from the village where no one could come across us or see us playing games they might not have understood. Because, apart from being unlike anyone in our family, Valeria was also unlike anyone in the village. And when she dived into the water, tracing a semicircle in the air, she looked more like a wild animal than a human being. That morning my brother drew her with a jaguar's body, her long hair flying in the wind. She burst out laughing. I was dumbstruck, though. It was exactly as I had imagined her as she was diving.

At lunch we were hungry for more news about the Wahyes-Wahno. We wanted to know what they ate and drank and what plants they used as medicines when they fell ill. We soon found out that almost everything in our part of the world has an equivalent in theirs. When Valeria had been crushing heads of garlic the night before she was trying to replicate the bo'o-ho or sacha garlic, a bush whose leaves are similar to our own common garlic. It is a master plant the properties of which include illuminating the mind and which the natives sometimes use as seasoning. Tristán also explained that in order to appreciate the sheer size and importance of the jungle we shouldn't look at it from the outside but, rather, from the inside, as if we had been born there and completely depended on it. Because the jungle was also a great workshop, a pharmacy, an inexhaustible larder in which we would always find food – the best-stocked warehouse in the world. The jungle protected us, cured our ailments, provided us with clothing, food, materials to build homes or weapons with which to defend ourselves. 'The jungle', he concluded 'is our Great Mother.'

I was fascinated as I listened to him, as I had been since we'd arrived there, but there was one thing I wasn't sure about, and this time I did feel comfortable asking. But before that I tried to sort out the facts in my head. Tristán and Valeria spent the whole day rekindling the memory of the Wahyes-Wahno. The first night Valeria managed to create a paste that reproduced the aroma of the jungle. The second night, crushing more and more garlic, she unsuccessfully tried to reproduce the smell of bo'o-ho, also known as sacha garlic, as it is similar to our own common garlic. To me that strange round trip seemed contradictory. Explorers, anthropologists or missionaries gave the name sacha garlic to a certain bush in the jungle because it reminded them of our own common garlic. And now our aunt and uncle were trying to make common garlic remind them of the leaves of a bush they'd known in the jungle. I never forgot that they were free, they didn't have any children, they spent their time travelling, they did whatever they wanted, and that's why people called them happy-go-lucky. So why did they shut themselves away in this village in the mountains if they wanted nothing more than to return to Amazonia? What was stopping them from going to live with the Wahyes-Wahno? Tristán burst out laughing, and, as he always did when he started laughing, he seemed even younger. And more handsome.

'We *do* live there,' he whispered in my ear. '*They* are here with us.' Then, almost immediately, he put his hands on my shoulders, looked me in the eyes and in the most natural voice in the world added, 'And with you, too. Or haven't you realized it yet?'

That night in the bar in the village square it seemed like the impossible was about to happen, and everyone went mad with their bets. A draw! The last coach of the day arrived. Three people and a dog got off, and when a couple, their daughter and a cat were preparing to get on, the cat escaped and ran off, and the girl refused to board without her cat. So three passengers and a dog disembarked but no one got on. 'Strange magic,' said the bar owner laughing as the villagers clicked their tongues or knocked back the last brandy. Valeria and Pedrito, the only ones who had bet on the passengers getting off, collected up their winnings: a few notes and a pile of coins that my brother jingled in his pocket the whole way back home. I hadn't placed a bet. Neither had Tristán. The two of us were lost in our own thoughts. For a few moments I liked to imagine that, through one of those strange coincidences that people put down to chance, we were both thinking the same thing. Because that afternoon my uncle had clearly included me in his world. I was still deeply moved, and more than anything I wanted him to be moved as well. But I looked at his face and had to discount the idea. He seemed worried. What's more, if I thought back to the moment I entered the bar I saw Tristán being handed a letter by the bar owner. In itself that wasn't of any importance, as all the villagers had their correspondence sent there. But now, looking back, I thought he looked upset, ill at ease, annoyed. Perhaps he even looked frightened, although that may be overstating it. Because my uncle had ripped open the envelope and started reading. Just for a few seconds. Then, as if worried that we would spot him, he glanced over to where Valeria, Pedrito and I were, turned his back on us and tore the letter into tiny pieces. At the time I thought nothing of it, but that scene, and especially Tristán's expression, had come back into my mind. It was just as he was looking now, opening the door to the house. Worried. Or concerned. I guessed that no map would be spread out over the table that night and that we wouldn't be chatting into the small hours accompanied by Valeria's percussion and the powerful aromas of garlic, earth, rotten fruit or stagnant water. 'I'm tired' was all he said after dinner. Pedrito yawned almost simultaneously.

'I don't want any milk tonight,' he said covering his mouth with his hand. 'Uncle Tristan, why do the Wahyes-Wahno speak the same as us if they are so different?'

Tristán looked at him questioningly. I understood immediately. My brother was wondering why, in such a far-off place, the natives use 'yes' for the affirmative and 'no' for the negative. Just like us. Sometimes Pedrito spoke my thoughts out loud before I could.

'Another day,' replied Tristán after a couple of seconds. 'Now, we need some sleep.'

My brother kicked me under the table.

'I don't think he knows,' he said under his breath.

Then he yawned again. I felt tired, too. But, as hard as I tried and with Pedrito already soundly asleep in his bed, that night it took me a while to drop off. Tristán and Valeria didn't stop their moaning and groaning and abandoned themselves to their games of love with more energy than ever. It was as if they hadn't seen each other for years or were afraid they would never see each other again for the rest of their lives. Or, it occurred to me, as if Tristán wanted to show Valeria that she was the only woman in the world for him.

Wah in the language of the Wahyes-Wahno means man or, to be more precise, *the man* or *the men*. There are many examples in the history of mankind – and Tristán told us a few – in which coincidence, error or mistakes have conspired to give names to lands or peoples that didn't belong to them until then. The history of the Spanish conquest of Latin America is full of them, and the history of the Wahyes-Wahno (although they have never been conquered or subjected by anyone) was no exception. They were *the men*, and that was enough for them. They didn't have many dealings with other peoples or tribes, but neither did their voluntary isolation exclude the possibility that at some point they might have been seen by groups of white people and might even have had sporadic contact. That's probably how some colonizer, researcher, timber or rubber merchant, together with missionaries and evangelists, must have taught them how to say yes and no.

Or being so intelligent and quick off the mark they worked it out themselves straight away. What happened is that they adopted the words 'yes' and 'no' and even expanded their implicit meanings of acceptance and rejection and started using them in their dealings with outsiders, always preceded by *Wah*: *Wahyessss* (that is, man accepts) or *Wahnoooo* (man rejects). Or, to put it another way, they, *the men*, started to judge outsiders on first appearances and act accordingly. And they cannot have liked the meddlesome visitors very much because they quickly became adept at camouflage, and their skill for passing unseen through the jungle was legendary. As their environment became deforested, the river waters polluted, the fish and plant life poisoned, they tirelessly searched for new areas to settle and reconstruct their villages. That was why – and here Tristán traced both his hands over the entire green map – it was impossible to know exactly where they were now. Survival had made nomads of them. They had become the almost invisible wanderers called the Wahyes-Wahno – or so the representatives of so-called civilization called this people about whom hardly anything was known. They were the Wahyes-Wahno for English speakers, the Wahsí-Wahno for Spanish speakers and Wahsim-Wahnão for Portuguese speakers. It was exactly the same thing.

'OK,' said Pedrito. And he shrugged his shoulders.

My brother was gradually losing interest in Tristán's passionate explanations but becoming more and more enthusiastic about Valeria's practical lessons: diving into the river, weaving branches or imitating the sounds made by the cats, dogs, goats, chickens and birds all around us. I had never seen him so happy or so involved. It was as if he were at summer school or summer camp. But as he spent more and more time in activities down by the river (not to mention hiking in the mountains hunting for animal tracks or droppings) I preferred to stay at home talking to Tristán and jotting down anything to do with the Wahyes-Wahno in my notebook. There were hardly any empty pages left, and I was delighted to see how much progress I had made since the first night when the real protagonists were the Pacahuara and the Wahyes-Wahno were just an unanswered question.

But now I did know all about them. And not only did I know all about them but I had a very special feeling, as if those marvellous people had been waiting for me since the day I was born and those lands were my true place of origin and my final destination. Tristán must have felt the same way when the woman in the jungle with the geometric markings on her face and two small babies in a sling accepted him without a word and gave him the warmest welcome. Because never, as far back as I could remember, had two simple words given me so much peace and happiness. I told Tristán about it. That's what I was experiencing at that time. Before I went to sleep I would whisper, 'Wahyes-Wahno', and immediately felt I was *there*, in a place that was familiar and surprising at the same time, surrounded by friendly faces, talking with my mind or listening to unspoken snatches of sage advice and revelations. And, more than anything else, *seeing*. Memories were filing past non-stop, and they were more vivid than ever. There were old memories, memories of memories and sometimes, more often than not, impossible memories. Because I could suddenly rekindle images that until that point I had known nothing about. The rites and observances of the tribe, for example, or the origin of the markings on the cheeks and foreheads of some of them, which – although they looked like drawings or tattoos – were simply the physical manifestation of certain feelings: love, hate, fear, annoyance, compassion and hospitality. The markings remained as long as the emotion causing them was experienced. And, in the same way that they appeared, they then faded away.

'It's another of their languages,' my uncle said one afternoon in the bar. 'Just another one, and it's almost as eloquent as words.'

But he didn't seem the slightest bit phased by what I'd just told him: that there is a space suspended in time that I could enter merely by closing my eyes and concentrating. It was quite the opposite. As if it were something we knew or had spoken about before. He just lit his pipe and whispered under his breath, 'Their wisdom will help you to solve many problems, although it'll always be you who comes up with the answer.' He blew out a series of smoke-rings aimed towards the ceiling. 'They are a state of mind. That's what they are. The Wahyes-Wahno are often a state of mind.'

We continued to go to the village square at the same time every day. We sometimes joined in with the game of betting on the passengers arriving and leaving. And other times we didn't even wait for the last coach. We had a drink, Tristán collected his correspondence, and we walked back home. I never saw him rip up a letter again, and I never again saw him looking worried or concerned. One of those afternoons when we were walking back home with Valeria and Pedrito a few steps behind us and were talking about everything and anything, I said to him, 'I dreamed about Aunt Berta today. When she was young. She was incredibly beautiful in my dream. And kind, too.'

My uncle burst out laughing. 'It wasn't a dream. Your Aunt

Berta really *was* incredibly beautiful, but she was a coward. She made her own bed . . .'

Later, when we were almost at the front door, while I was trying to make some sense out of what he'd said, he slapped me on the back.

'Cowardice or excessive caution – which is the same thing – always turns against the coward. Never forget that.' Then his face contorted just as it had when he ripped the letter into little pieces thinking no one could see him. But he wasn't thinking about Aunt Berta any more. I was certain of that. Just as I was certain that, because of an unexpected association of ideas, he'd been gripped by an old fear. He glanced behind where, a few metres away, Valeria and my brother were collecting stones on the path and, making sure they couldn't hear us, he whispered, 'And jealousy. Never forget that either.'

Mum still phoned every night. Always at the same time. She spoke to Tristán first and then to us, although, as her voice reached into the furthest corners of the house, the three of us heard the same news at the same time. The great news was that Dad was definitely getting better. It started to become old news because every day Mum enthusiastically told all three of us about it. She told Tristán first, then me and finally Pedrito. Before saying goodbye she always remembered to send her love to Valeria and say how grateful she was to her for having us. And Valeria, from the kitchen or the bedroom, from whichever room she was in, arched her eyebrows and shook her head smiling. 'But I love having them here.'

One day there was a different kind of telephone call. It wasn't at the usual time, and no one, apart from our mother, had ever phoned our aunt and uncle since we'd been at their house. I ran down the corridor, somewhat concerned. Valeria was holding the telephone and talking loudly. 'Yes? Hello? Who is it?' She smiled when she saw me, shrugged and was about to hang up when the two of us clearly heard that the person at the other end had already done so. There were more calls on different days and at different times. I rushed to answer the telephone on a number of occasions, but all I heard was the familiar silence and the dialling tone as the phone was put down at the other end. It was annoying and disheartening. It wasn't a wrong number, the telephone wasn't out of order and it wasn't a joke. But those silent calls could not be a good omen. Or, worse, something not good at all, something decidedly nefarious or unhealthy, perhaps irrational, was incubating feverishly in the midst of our peaceful summer. And it was easy to detect it in Valeria's increasingly bad mood and in Tristán's offhand manner. Because Tristán didn't seem the least bit worried by the telephone ringing at any time of day or night, and that when you picked it up there was no one there. He was so indifferent and so clearly wanted to show that he, Tristán, wasn't at all worried about what was going on that I suspected that actually the opposite was true. And I put two and two together. In fact, I didn't even need to do that because the few pieces of the jigsaw I could see had joined themselves up all on their own: the ripped-up letter, Tristán looking half worried and half suspicious or his mentioning jealousy a few days before on the way home. It was as if he were rekindling some tempestuous event from the past and was worried that it would happen again.

I saw it all the more clearly in bed that night, just before going to sleep, when I whispered 'Wahyes-Wahno' and all the day's events came rushing back into my mind. I had a whole jumble of images in my head: snippets of the evening in the kitchen and things that the family had said about Tristán that I must have once heard, but it was only now that they took on an unexpected meaning. And I felt I was able to put a name to the strange situation we were experiencing. It was a triviality, a trifle that could, all the same, end in disaster. Because, with a good sense that was unusual for the age I was at the time, I understood something that life taught me later on with many different examples: an argument, an outburst, some kind of breakdown is often caused by an event that would have no meaning on its own unless it linked back to others that did mean something at the time. And that's what happened with the telephone calls, or the letter, or Tristán's apprehension. Time was turning back on itself and everything was happening all over again. The reason my uncle ripped up the letter and said nothing to Valeria was because he was scared of how she would react. Jealousy. An unhealthy passion that perhaps made Tristán hide away in a lost village in the mountains. I was prepared to walk over coals for my uncle. *This time*, at least, he was innocent, and it was only his past, his happy past that the family had sometimes talked about, that was to blame for the confusion. Now his past was determined to return at the most inappropriate time. My mother said that Tristán had broken many hearts. But that was before, before he had met Valeria, I couldn't have been more certain of it. He respected Valeria and loved her dearly. And he also, and I only realized this now, protected her and looked after her in his own way. That was why he tried to keep her away from anything that might upset her. As if, in spite of her apparent strength, she were just a little girl. As if she were ill.

*

I didn't have to wait long for my suspicions to be confirmed. One night, shortly after Mum's usual call, the telephone rang again. This time Tristán answered it. I remember he said 'Yes, what's up?' completely naturally, probably thinking it was his sister again and that she'd forgotten to tell him something. But there was silence this time, too. It was a dense, threatening silence that made my uncle's face contort and to which I listened at one end of the corridor almost without breathing. I wanted him to hang up. For him to hang up once and for all or for the mysterious presence at the other end of the line to beat him to it and hang up first, as they usually did. But he hesitated. Perhaps it was deliberate – as if, tired of the whole situation, he wanted the inevitable to happen as soon as possible.

And the inanity, the trifle, the event that had no importance whatsoever on its own, occurred in the blink of an eye. The ancient telephone rang out like a powerful radio, and the sweet, whispering voice of a woman could be heard in all four corners of the house. I didn't understand a thing she was saying. I couldn't understand Tristán either when he interrupted her in an unexpectedly furious voice that frightened me. I couldn't understand a single word of the argument and, to this day, have no idea what language they were speaking. But the inflection in their voices left no room for doubt. She was asking and he was refusing; she was suggesting something and he was rejecting it. Her insistence just made him more annoyed. And in the end, even though it was abundantly clear that he, Tristán, wanted nothing whatsoever to do with the owner of that sweet, whispering voice, he shouted out loud, as loud as in the theatre. And in our own language. So that we would all understand.

'Don't call again! Forget all about us!'
But the poison had already been injected.

There are many things I will never know. Who that woman was, for example, or what must have happened in the past to make the situation so unbearable now; and whether it was always the same woman or whether there were several. The only thing I do know is that things quickly came to a head. Valeria started drinking. She was really knocking it back. I left her in the kitchen with a bottle of wine that had just been opened, and when I returned ten minutes later the bottle was almost empty. You could tell there would be no dinner that night – certainly not a calm and peaceful dinner as usual. Tristán had put some bread, cheese and salami on the table. I wasn't hungry any more.

'Isn't it all lovely?' said Valeria suddenly, looking at us with blurry eyes. 'Don't believe a word your uncle tells you!' She was talking in a shaky voice and stumbling over her words like a drunk in a film. I avoided looking at Tristán. 'I'll tell you the sad truth, children.' She repeated the word 'children', burst out laughing and spread out the green map that had accompanied so many of our evenings together on the table.

I made a sign to Pedrito. We had to go to bed. As soon as possible.

'No way.' Now Valeria was shaking her finger at us. 'Stay here, keep quiet and listen to what I have to say.'

I had never wanted anything so much: to melt away, to disappear and leave them in the kitchen. But there was no way of escaping what was about to happen. My aunt downed the rest of the bottle in one long gulp, stood up and scratched at the map. For a moment her fingers seemed like claws and her laughter reminded me of a hyena. I thought she was ill. Really ill.

'The Wahyes-Wahno don't exist!'

She said it slowly, enjoying how the words sounded, speaking with deliberate exaggeration and to one person alone: Tristán. This time I couldn't avoid looking at him. His face was red, and there was a throbbing vein on his forehead.

'Everything's in that little head,' she continued. 'A fifth-rate anthropologist. Old wives' tales that only children would believe.'

I took my brother's arm, and we left them on their own. Pedrito followed me without a murmur. We went to our room, and I bolted the door. This was serious, very serious. Perhaps that's why, to calm my brother down or to fool myself, I whispered, 'It's just a lovers' tiff.'

We heard glass smashing and crockery being thrown against the wall or on the floor. We heard cooking pots sounding like funeral bells. And insults. So many insults and mutual accusations. There were screams that cut through the air like arrows, increasingly wounding and forceful. I thought that something irrevocable was about to happen. So, I did it. I still don't know how I managed it. I shouted with all my strength. It was more like a wild animal than a human being. It was a shriek from the very depths of my being. It was a shot that went in through your ears and pierced your heart. I shouted, 'WAH-NOOOOOOOOO!'

And the voices stopped immediately.

I was panting for breath and had almost no puff left. I felt shocked and liberated at the same time. I was breathing in the dense silence that had suddenly fallen over the house. All I could hear was my own panting and Pedrito's breathing and heartbeat. A few seconds later I wrapped his arms around my waist, and we stayed like that for a long time. Until he fell asleep.

I started packing my bag. My brother was still asleep, and there wasn't any sound from the rest of the house. Perhaps that's why a faint metallic noise took me so much by surprise. I turned off the light and looked out of the window. Valeria was at the garage door struggling with the lock. Her hair was loose, she had a mac around her shoulders and the only other thing she was wearing was the wrap she'd worn to swim in the river. It was tied around her waist. In the moonlight I thought I could see markings on her face, drawings. I leaned over the windowsill. Her face and part of her body were covered in geometric shapes. But they looked nothing like those I had imagined on Tristán's indigenous saviour. They were aggressive and bloodthirsty, as if they had just been hammered out. And if they did say anything at all, if it were a language as I had been given to understand during our days together, they communicated anger, indignation, instability. She finally went into the garage, and I waited. A few minutes later the old van's headlights lit up the countryside and were immediately lost on the road.

I switched on the light and carried on collecting up my things. Those days full of discovery were already part of the past. But I didn't want to think about that or be sad.

A short while afterwards I heard footsteps in the corridor. I waited and recognized my mother's voice. 'What's going on, Tristán? Has something happened?'

From our room you could hear the voice on the telephone more clearly than Tristán's. I opened the door a crack. Now my uncle was apologizing for calling so late.

'Something's come up. More of an opportunity than a problem. We're leaving on a trip. Tomorrow.'

I heard silence. A long silence. And I'm choosing my words carefully. That's what I heard. Silence could be heard just as much, or more, than words on that telephone.

'You've had another row with Valeria, haven't you?'

I closed the door. Tristán was a bad liar. A really bad liar. And Mum must have known about the quarrels that her brother and his wife had. I wasn't interested in whatever else they had to say. We would go back home the next day on the first coach. That was the last thing I heard Tristán say. And that was what I had decided a short while ago, nothing more and nothing less.

'I hope the children haven't been a pain.'

That was when the best summer of my life came to an end, unexpectedly and abruptly. I closed my suitcase, then shut Pedrito's and sat down on the bed.

A few hours later Tristán knocked on the door. He had the same clothes on as the night before, his hair was unkempt and he smelled of wine. For the first time he looked old. To a thirteen-year-old girl a fifty-year-old man is old. I felt sorry for him, really sorry for him. He looked at me, trying to act as if nothing had happened. But he wasn't even surprised that our bags were packed.

Valeria didn't like goodbyes and even less so if woken up when she was fast asleep. What's more, she'd had indigestion the night before and needed to rest. But he promised that as soon as they got to America they would send us postcards. Understood?

'From Brazil, Peru, Ecuador, Colombia, Venezuela,' he said. I couldn't look at him.

We walked along the road like three shadows, as if there were nothing to bind us together. My brother was still half asleep and cross about not saying goodbye to Valeria. Tristán was breathing like an asthmatic and had withdrawn into stony silence after his torrent of excuses and lies. I was listening to the silence again and wondering about a whole host of things for which there would never be an answer. I took a deep breath when we reached the village square. The bar was opening up, and the owner, with a broom in his hand, looked at us and couldn't hide his surprise. 'What's going on?' he asked staring at our bags. None of us bothered to reply, but I was glad that the bar was open and that the owner was there. Just like any other morning when nothing out of the ordinary had happened. Tristán remembered that we hadn't had any breakfast and sat us at a table with two chairs and ordered a couple of pastries. Then he leaned against the bar and downed a brandy in one go.

'What's indigestion?' asked Pedrito.

'What Valeria had yesterday,' I answered without looking at him and keeping my eye on the bar. 'It's an illness you get better from straight away.'

My brother was furious.

'It's all his fault,' he said pointing at Tristán. 'Everything he told us was lies. He's treated us like small children.'

He took a drawing book out of his bag and ripped out a page I immediately recognized. It was Valeria, half-woman, half-jaguar, diving into the river.

'I don't want any of the others,' he said.

He was about to rip up the drawing book, but I stopped him. We quarrelled. He ended up giving in and, shrugging, put the only sheet of paper he wanted in his pocket. I thought of Aunt

Berta, my scrapbook and our argument. This situation seemed somewhat similar: some drawings, someone wanting to rip them up and the other person trying to stop them. But now, as in those periods of drowsiness I had told my uncle about, I understood everything. And I saw Berta when she was young, incredibly beautiful and in love with a fascinating and adventurous Tristán. She was ecstatic, mad about him but too attached to her own sense of security to accept any other way of life. And that's what had caused the bitterness and hatred, her inability to contain herself when, years later, she recognized the same emotions in her own niece. She had destroyed her future by being a coward. 'Excessive caution,' I remembered. Something I would never forget. Just as I would never forget Valeria and her terrible affliction: jealousy.

I went over to Tristán with the drawing book under my arm. He had another glass of brandy in front of him, but I pretended I hadn't noticed. I needed him to clear things up for me. To clear up whether there was any truth in what Valeria had said or if what she'd said was simply an explosion, revenge, an outburst of anger when terrible things are said that haven't entered our heads before. I also wanted to know where she could have gone off to so angrily and why I'd seen strange markings and geometric shapes on her body in the moonlight. More than anything else, the most important thing I wanted to know was whether the Wahyes-Wahno existed or not.

I didn't get to ask anything. When Tristán saw me, he clicked his tongue several times and shook his head. I realized he was asking me to keep quiet. I also realized, although his lips hadn't moved, that he knew exactly what I was thinking.

'No,' he said. 'Not you.'

He took a deep breath, put his hands on my shoulders and looked me straight in the eyes.

'Your brother's still young and he'll forget, but you won't. You've been among *them*. And *they* accepted you. From the start.'

I think he smiled. I'm not sure. At that moment the bar owner announced that the coach had arrived, and I felt happy and sad all at the same time. I wanted to laugh and to cry and, more than anything, I really wanted my uncle to carry on talking and not to stop talking as we walked to the coach and not to stop until the driver started the coach up. But it didn't turn out exactly that way.

'You've got the keys to a secret world,' he said in a soft voice. 'Enjoy it. And if one day you want to share it, then share it, but choose who you share it with carefully.'

His last words sounded sad to me. Then, speaking in a louder voice, he said he didn't like goodbyes either. He slapped Pedrito on the back and leaned back on the bar again. My brother and I picked up our luggage, boarded the coach, sat down in the front row and waited. I didn't know if it was the best or the saddest day of my whole life. My brother stifled a yawn, and I began leafing mechanically through the drawing book. There was Tristán, lost in the jungle, bare-chested with the red bandanna around his head. There was the woman who saved him with the two babies in the sling around her neck; the village he was taken to; the natives' faces looking at the injured man; arrows flying through the air; members of the tribe at the point of melting into the trees, changing colour, changing their appearance, disappearing into lakes and swamps or becoming one with the luxuriance of their immense green world. The huge funnel. And it was more than strange. Those sheets of paper that Pedrito no longer wanted, those faces, that vegetation and the villages in the drawings were almost exactly the same as I had imagined them. I was going to tell him. I was going to ask him why he had thought of tying a red bandanna around our uncle's head or why he had drawn a gigantic funnel using every shade of green. It was the same bandanna I had given him, and they were the same concentric circles I was scared of being swallowed up by while I was *seeing* through Tristán's eyes. But I never managed to get a word out this time either. Pedrito had just fallen asleep on my shoulder. I did my best to make him comfortable on the two seats. I put a jumper under his head and sat down in the seat behind next to the window. Then I discovered it. The driver had just closed the luggage compartment and was handing some baskets and a package to an elderly couple waiting on the pavement. Now I remembered the scene of just a few minutes before. Two passengers were getting off. And two passengers were getting on! An elderly married couple and my brother and me. Two for two. It was a draw. Pedrito was asleep, the bar owner hadn't realized either and Tristán, who was leaving the bar just then, without looking at us, was turning towards the path that would take him home. I ran to the back seat and rapped on the rear window. Although I knew he couldn't hear me, I shouted, 'A draw! It's a draw!' The coach started off, and Tristán, still with his back to me, as if guessing I was calling out to him, raised his right hand in farewell. Then he stumbled along the path until he disappeared around a bend.

I would never see either of them again. I already knew that when I was at the rear window of the coach. I knew – or rather I *saw* – just as I did in those periods of drowsiness wandering through different times and recognizing places I'd never been. In my mind I could also read some letters that still hadn't been written. Short letters sent to the family, written by both of them from far-off places. Letters that one day would stop arriving without anyone being in the least bit concerned. I heard the words 'Go with the flow!' again as my parents smiled and shook their heads and Aunt Berta pursed her lips in a rictus grin full of bitterness. I wasn't surprised when I saw the adult Pedrito, now an architect, very serious and formal, picking up some plans from his desk and the Valeria-Jaguar drawing, slightly yellowed with age, in a frame on one of the walls of his studio. But, more than anything, I felt that I was my own person; I was *me*. I was at the rear window of the coach stretching out the last moments of that summer and experiencing a strange emotion I couldn't quite explain. It was a sad happiness or a happy sadness. And, once again, I wanted to burst out laughing and burst into tears as well. I was euphoric and dejected all at the same time, and now that I'm the same age as my aunt and uncle must have been back then I remember it was a deep and intense feeling. I was a thirteen-year-old girl, and I'd fallen deeply and passionately in love with Tristán. And although I didn't know that that first love was an impossible love, I did know that it was mutual. Because with my face still at the window, without being able to see anything but the dust raised up by the coach on the road, I had no doubt whatsoever. I had given him my admiration, all my affection, the intense dreams of a teenager. And, in turn, he had left me his most precious asset as a legacy. The fabulous and secret world of the Wahyes-Wahno.

SOME AUTHORS WE HAVE PUBLISHED

James Agee • Bella Akhmadulina • Tariq Ali • Kenneth Allsop • Alfred Andersch
Guillaume Apollinaire • Machado de Assis • Miguel Angel Asturias • Duke of Bedford
Oliver Bernard • Thomas Blackburn • Jane Bowles • Paul Bowles • Richard Bradford
Ilse, Countess von Bredow • Lenny Bruce • Finn Carling • Blaise Cendrars • Marc Chagall
Giorgio de Chirico • Uno Chiyo • Hugo Claus • Jean Cocteau • Albert Cohen
Colette • Ithell Colquhoun • Richard Corson • Benedetto Croce • Margaret Crosland
e.e. cummings • Stig Dalager • Salvador Dalí • Osamu Dazai • Anita Desai
Charles Dickens • Bernard Diederich • Fabián Dobles • William Donaldson
Autran Dourado • Yuri Druzhnikov • Lawrence Durrell • Isabelle Eberhardt
Sergei Eisenstein • Shusaku Endo • Erté • Knut Faldbakken • Ida Fink
Wolfgang George Fischer • Nicholas Freeling • Philip Freund • Carlo Emilio Gadda
Rhea Galanaki • Salvador Garmendia • Michel Gauquelin • André Gide
Natalia Ginzburg • Jean Giono • Geoffrey Gorer • William Goyen • Julien Gracq
Sue Grafton • Robert Graves • Angela Green • Julien Green • George Grosz
Barbara Hardy • H.D. • Rayner Heppenstall • David Herbert • Gustaw Herling
Hermann Hesse • Shere Hite • Stewart Home • Abdullah Hussein • King Hussein of Jordan
Ruth Inglis • Grace Ingoldby • Yasushi Inoue • Hans Henny Jahnn • Karl Jaspers
Takeshi Kaiko • Jaan Kaplinski • Anna Kavan • Yasunuri Kawabata • Nikos Kazantzakis
Orhan Kemal • Christer Kihlman • James Kirkup • Paul Klee • James Laughlin
Patricia Laurent • Violette Leduc • Lee Seung-U • Vernon Lee • József Lengyel
Robert Liddell • Francisco García Lorca • Moura Lympany • Thomas Mann
Dacia Maraini • Marcel Marceau • André Maurois • Henri Michaux • Henry Miller
Miranda Miller • Marga Minco • Yukio Mishima • Quim Monzó • Margaret Morris
Angus Wolfe Murray • Atle Næss • Gérard de Nerval • Anaïs Nin • Yoko Ono
Uri Orlev • Wendy Owen • Arto Paasilinna • Marco Pallis • Oscar Parland
Boris Pasternak • Cesare Pavese • Milorad Pavic • Octavio Paz • Mervyn Peake
Carlos Pedretti • Dame Margery Perham • Graciliano Ramos • Jeremy Reed
Rodrigo Rey Rosa • Joseph Roth • Ken Russell • Marquis de Sade • Cora Sandel
Iván Sándor • George Santayana • May Sarton • Jean-Paul Sartre
Ferdinand de Saussure • Gerald Scarfe • Albert Schweitzer
George Bernard Shaw • Isaac Bashevis Singer • Patwant Singh • Edith Sitwell
Suzanne St Albans • Stevie Smith • C.P. Snow • Bengt Söderbergh
Vladimir Soloukhin • Natsume Soseki • Muriel Spark • Gertrude Stein • Bram Stoker
August Strindberg • Rabindranath Tagore • Tambimuttu • Elisabeth Russell Taylor
Emma Tennant • Anne Tibble • Roland Topor • Miloš Urban • Anne Valery
Peter Vansittart • José J. Veiga • Tarjei Vesaas • Noel Virtue • Max Weber
Edith Wharton • William Carlos Williams • Phyllis Willmott
G. Peter Winnington • Monique Wittig • A.B. Yehoshua • Marguerite Young
Fakhar Zaman • Alexander Zinoviev • Emile Zola

 Peter Owen Publishers, 81 Ridge Road, London N8 9NP, UK
T + 44 (0)20 8350 1775 / E info@peterowen.com
www.peterowen.com / @PeterOwenPubs
Independent publishers since 1951